# AWAY WITH HIM
*Swept Away, Book 2*
ROSEMARY WILLHIDE

Inside their little bubble, newly engaged, Nia Kelly and Derek Pierce, are blissfully happy. Their passion reaches new heights as they explore each other in sensual, wicked ways.

Unfortunately, the rest of the world has not received the memo. They are hit with a barrage of attacks from Nia's past and Derek's pressure-filled Hollywood career. Their happiness and future are in peril at every turn.

Derek is steadfast in his commitment to Nia. No matter what, he will never let go. Nia is his and Derek is hers—they belong together.

Nia prays their love is enough. With everything she has, she holds on and vows not to run away. It's a promise she hopes she can keep.

# AWAY WITH HIM
## Swept Away, Book 2

# ROSEMARY WILLHIDE

**LUMINOSITY PUBLISHING LLP**

AWAY WITH HIM
*Swept Away, Book 2*
Copyright © March 2015 RosemaryWillhide
Paperback ISBN: 978-1-910397-60-2

Cover Art by Poppy Designs

# Dedication

This book is dedicated to my parents, Charles and Dorothy Willhide. Thank you for your unwavering support in my creative endeavors, especially this one. You're the coolest parents ever. I love you. This one's for you, but if you read it, you will probably have to go to confession.

# Chapter One

"Derek, put me down," I screamed.

The love of my life hoisted me over his shoulder and was about to throw me into the pool, the deep end.

"You've kept me waiting long enough, fiancée. It's time to take the plunge, Nia."

It was all fun and games up to this moment. "I can't swim."

"More excuses? I'm not falling for that."

"I really can't. I can't swim!"

Derek put me down immediately. His hands cupped my face. "Are you serious? Why didn't you tell me?"

I looked down and mumbled, "It's kind of embarrassing. I don't want to talk about it."

His finger tucked under my chin and tilted my face to meet his gaze. "Nia, look at me. It's no big deal. Let me teach you."

I couldn't deal with this right now. We were on such a high after our engagement last night. Everything was perfect. Last night was perfect. Our love was perfect, and our new little puppy, Molly, was perfect too.

I hatched a plan, and shimmied toward the oversized lounge chair by the shallow end of the pool.

I ripped off my bikini top. "You've taught me many naughty things. I'd like another one of those lessons. I'm a very eager student."

Derek had that look. I was in the clear. As he drew closer, I fondled my breasts and slid my hands to my bikini bottoms. He placed his hands on top of mine. "Allow me, I insist."

He guided them down slow. There I was naked in our backyard on this beautiful June afternoon. We were in our "bubble" and I was the happiest woman on earth.

My body ached for his. By the size of his growing erection, I'd say he ached too. As he yanked me close, my breath hitched, and as his hands gripped my ass. I floated my fingers down the ridges of his sculpted chest and onto my sex.

I whispered, "You see this, it needs a lot of attention." I dipped a finger inside myself. "It's very needy."

He smiled in that devious way. Took the errant finger and licked off my juices. "I think you mean greedy. You have a very greedy pussy. Maybe it needs a spanking."

*Holy shit!* Spanking my pussy? Was that a thing?

Derek spread a towel over the lounge chair, and stripped off his swim trunks. Just the sight of his chiseled, naked body gleaming in the sun was enough to turn me on. My fiancé was hotter than hell. Sometimes it was still hard to believe he was mine.

"Nia, lie down and spread your legs for me. I need

to teach that greedy pussy a lesson."

School was back in session and my teacher's gracious plenty cast quite a shadow. He coasted his beautiful hands up my inner thighs and opened me.

His tongue licked up and down my greedy cunt. He was the Michelangelo of pussy, a true artist. The way he worked me, slow and easy, caused my entire body to shudder. He lavished me with sultry flicks, and long, luxurious strokes. At just the precise moment, he sucked my clit into his wet, hungry mouth. I gripped the cushions and gasped in pleasure. Two fingers pushed inside, granting me a barrage of rampant thrusts. I wriggled under his sensual attack. The palm of his hand splayed on my belly, securing me in place. Together his mouth and thrusting digits propelled me to the edge.

Derek kissed my mound. "You're close, aren't you?"

Like the bad girl I was, I shoved his face back into my sex. "Yes, Derek, oh God, so close."

He grabbed my wrists, leaving me empty and wanting.

I begged. "Please don't stop."

"I'm not stopping, but I am going to punish your greedy pussy. You both need discipline."

Using two fingers, Derek spread my cunt lips wide, exposing my vulnerable, glistening clit. A sudden series of taps landed on my sex. *Zippity fucking do da!* This was an entirely new titillating sensation. Slowly the taps grew faster and fiercer. He was indeed spanking my pussy. An orgasm built, but it felt different. He was taking my body some place it had never been before. A thunderous pressure boomed within. Then, it happened —I squirted! Not just a little, but a lot. I was like the freaking fountains at Bellagio! What was my body doing? I clasped Derek's shoulders as my rigorous release burst forth.

He said in a husky low tone, "That's it, God, I love it."

A final rush flew out of my body. I was breathless and covered in sweat, lying in a puddle of me. Derek handed me another towel. The one beneath me was soaked. We cuddled up on the chair together. He held me like always. Neither one of us uttered a word, but he wore a satisfied grin.

Finally, I responded, "So, that was different."

"Different in a good way or bad way?"

"Different in a great way. I think I invented a new amusement park ride. 'Escape to Splash Mountain.'"

He threw his head back and laughed. Then the corners of his mouth upturned in that sexy way. "Do you think your greedy pussy learned its lesson?"

"Not yet, teacher. It wants extra credit."

He ran his thumb across my lower lip, and brought his mouth down on mine. His kisses grew urgent as he angled my hips to straddle him.

"I loved making you come like that. I want to do it again."

I didn't know if I had it in me, but I wasn't about to

argue. My greedy pussy spearheaded his throbbing erection inside. An instant moan escaped from us. I careened up and down his colossal cock. He felt incredible, filling me to capacity. I couldn't get enough of him. The way he looked at me made me feel like the sexiest creature on earth.

Derek breathed heavy and groaned. "Ah, sweetie, you're amazing."

"Amazingly naughty."

"Show me. Let me see how naughty you really are."

I sat upright, proud of the show I was about to perform for him. I ran my hands through my long dark locks and let them fall around my shoulders. He feasted his eyes on my small swelled breasts. I licked my fingers and circled my pert hardening nipples.

He grinned in delight. "Good girl."

I garnered more praise when I pinched them and accelerated our pace. My pussy swallowed him inside and treated his dick to a prime shafting. I danced up and down his pleasure pole like a wanton stripper soaking in the limelight.

I slowed and teased my clit with my hand. "You're right. This does need to be taught a lesson." My head fell back as I shamelessly fingered myself to the brink.

Derek grasped my hand. "The show's over. I'm in charge of making my pussy come. He crushed me to his chest and reclaimed possession of me. Our lips united in desperation as our tongues swirled together in a crazed passion. I grabbed onto his dark-blond hair accepting the demanding commands of his hungry mouth. He bent his knees and riveted me with an onslaught of powerful strokes.

His hand captured my chin. "Sweetie, look at me. Remember when I said it was only the beginning and from now on I'm going to fuck you harder than ever before?"

I heaved. "Yes."

"Are you ready?"

"Yes."

With one swift motion, he flipped me onto my back, and pressed my knees against my chest. He took control of his pussy and me. His hardness sank inside me to his balls, repeatedly, making my walls rumble around him. I reveled in his reckless strokes, pounding me to the hilt. *Oh, Fuck!* That new sensation hit me without warning. My liquid sex poured. It was so intense. There was nothing to do, but give in, let go, and shriek like a mad woman.

Derek growled. "That's it, baby. Shower my cock with your cum."

With one more set of conquering thrusts, he released his hot load inside me.

Derek wiped the sweat off his brow, lay down next to me and drew me close. We were a hot, wet mess, but it was divine.

Once the thumping of my heart quieted, I said, "I think you finally did it. You've officially worn me out.

That was like the trifecta of orgasms."

His lips brushed my forehead. "Do you have any idea how much I love you?"

"Do you have any idea how soaked we are?"

"It's a perfect time for a dip in the pool?" I shot him a disapproving glare and sat up. He grabbed my hand. "Relax, you are literally 'saved by the bell,' my business manager, Don, is going to be here soon."

*What?* We were going to work with Molly on basic obedience, have dinner and watch a new summer series on TV. This business manager was never in the plan. He should know by now, don't change the freaking plan.

"Why is your business manager coming? I thought we had a plan."

"Look, I know I'm springing this on you, but it's a good thing. I called Don this morning and asked to set up a meeting with the three of us. It turns out he was flying to Vegas today, so he's coming here before he begins his vacation."

This made no sense. Why would I need to meet with business manager Don? Before I could say a word, Molly trotted toward us followed by an entire roll of unraveling toilet paper. Our little black puppy was up from her nap and curious. We cracked up. She had this precious expression on her face that said, "Hey, Mom and Dad. Look what I can do." Derek picked her up and carried her back to the house, while I gathered the toilet paper.

"Nia, I want you to trust me. Don coming here today is a good thing."

"Of course I trust you. I will take a shower and meet this Don."

* * * *

"This is everything I could get together at the last minute." Don Clark placed file after file on the dining room table in a rather specific order. He was in his early forties and bore a striking resemblance to the angry Lollipop Guild. Except for the thick head of brown hair, he could have been one of them.

Derek was perfectly relaxed, excited in fact. I was uncomfortable. There was something a little too formal about the dining room. Sitting there with Don made it worse. I got the impression he didn't approve of me.

Derek picked up a folder in the middle of his neatly arranged pile and Don let out a sigh of exasperation.

"Sorry, did you have these in order?" Derek asked.

Don replied in a sheepish manner, "It's not you. It's me. My wife calls me a control freak."

My mouth dropped open and I smiled at Derek.

Don continued, "I tell her, I'm not a control freak, I'm a control enthusiast."

"A control enthusiast?" I exclaimed. "I love it! Don, you are so speaking my language."

I was more at ease, since we found a common ground. He showed me the content of the mystery folders. It was all of Derek's assets. *Holy cash cow!* My soon-to-be husband was a financial genius. Derek was part owner of successful restaurants and small businesses. He had a producer credit for a movie franchise that continued to rake in big bucks. That was just the tip of the money iceberg. Maybe it wasn't the norm for every actor to have a huge estate and a plane, unless the actor was Derek Pierce. Everything he touched turned to gold and silver. I went right back to being uncomfortable.

I glanced down at the documents. "Derek, can I talk to you a minute, in the kitchen?"

We excused ourselves and hurried to the kitchen.

Derek took my hands in his. "Sweetie, you look upset. What's wrong?"

"I'm not upset. I just don't understand why you had Don come with all your files. Couldn't you have told me about it yourself?"

"He's here so we can add your name to all my assets. I told you last night, everything I have is for you. I want to take care of you."

"I thought he was coming so I could sign a prenup. I totally will. You've worked so hard for everything. This just doesn't feel right. I'm not your wife yet."

"You think I want you to sign a prenup?"

"I assumed I would be."

"That's the furthest thing from my mind. You are mine and I am yours. Isn't that what you want?"

"Yes, it's just that—"

"It's too much and it freaks you out." Derek finished my sentence for me. I peeked up at him and nodded. He wrapped his arms around me and rubbed my back. "Okay, I get it. I've really got to learn to quit springing things on you."

"Yep. That would be a great day. Can you tell me when it's going to happen, so I can plan?"

He chuckled. "I will have to get back to you on that, Miss Kelly. Let's go tell Don to start his vacation. I'm sure there's a blackjack table on the strip with his name on it."

We said our goodbyes to Don and resumed our originally scheduled plan. We worked with Molly in the backyard on "sit" and "down." She got the hang of it, but it bothered me she gravitated toward the pool. Perhaps we should've started with "no" and "come."

We sat down to our baby broccoli and grilled chicken, marinated in a little soy sauce, garlic, ginger, with a hint of orange juice.

Then we made some calls to share our good news. As expected Derek's parents, and Aunt Mary Jane and Uncle Bill were ecstatic about our engagement. Derek also called his publicist. Aaron told Derek it might be a good idea to announce it ourselves, so we could control the story. If we tried too hard to keep it a secret, it would create more interest in our personal lives.

* * * *

We watched our programs like *Ma and Pa Kettle,* snuggled up on the couch. I only had one more day with Derek before he had to leave on a publicity tour for the week. He was flying to New York City to promote *First Bite* and the ensemble comedy *Fourth of July*. It was one of those star-studded blockbusters—pick a holiday; a group of A-list actors and boom, mayhem ensued. Derek was more excited about the independent film called *Traitors in Our Midst*. It was a spy thriller, full of suspense and intrigue.

After Molly scampered out for a potty, the three of us headed upstairs. When I came out of the bathroom, Derek was waiting for me in bed with his familiar devilish grin.

I straddled him. "What's that look for?"

He smoothed my hair. "I was just thinking we've been engaged one whole day. We should probably celebrate."

"Did you want to celebrate in my mouth?"

He chuckled, while his blue eyes gleamed. "My dear fiancée, that is an excellent idea."

It was only fair he'd have some extra attention after what I experienced earlier in the day. I was more than happy to please him. I headed south to his tasty swell of cock flesh. My tongue sampled his delicious dick causing it to strain and stretch to its complete veiny, magnitude. I lightly grazed my fingers up and down and watched him squirm. My soft, wet mouth took his tip inside.

He hissed. "Oh God, Nia, yes."

My taste buds came alive with a small drip of his honeyed pre-cum. I swallowed the savory morsel and descended to his root. Sucking in a breath, I embedded him in the back of my throat. I loved this. His muscled frame writhed under my deep, slippery spell.

He gently eased me off him. "I want to taste you. Bring your greedy little pussy up here."

Was he talking about sixty-nine? I called it, "the number thing." I'd never done it before, so I ramped up my throat fucking efforts. "Um…that's okay. I'm good."

Derek reached for my hand. "Nia, look at me. What's wrong?"

"Nothing's wrong, I just haven't ever…you know, sat there…on your facial area."

He bit the side of his mouth to keep from laughing. My hands flew to my face in embarrassment, and he removed them. "Come here, sweetie. Just so were clear, after all the things we've done together, you're going to draw the line at my facial area?"

"No, it's not that. I do want to do that with you, or I did. I'm just worried because of what happened earlier with the fountain-like situation… You might drown."

Derek let out a huge guttural laugh. "God, I love you." He caressed my face and swept me away with sweet, tender kisses.

He pressed his forehead to mine. "Just so you're clear, the reason I wanted you on my facial area was because I was hoping you'd have a fountain-like situation. I want to drink you in, every last drop."

*Son of a bitch.* The way he said it, it sounded so hot. Nervousness be damned. I was so going to sit on his face.

Derek upped the ante. "I have a proposition for you. If I make you come first, I get something I want, and if you make me come first, you get something you want."

I hooked my arms around his neck. "So it's a competition? Hmm… I'm very competitive, Mr. Pierce. You may have met your match."

"You think so? We'll see. Climb aboard my future bride."

Everything stirred within me, as Derek took my hand, and anchored me in place. Oh, my God, I was really doing it, sixty-nine—the number thing. My pussy rested on his face. From the first stroke of his expert tongue, I was in trouble. This was pure hedonistic pleasure, and so fucking salacious. I almost forgot it was a competition. My worthy opponent was a gold medal pussy eater. I relished every lick and flicker of his tasting talents.

We were indeed doing the number thing, but just me. Before I unraveled, I had to take my mind off this lustful gratification and concentrate on besting his cock. I lifted my head and realized I'd been bamboozled. Derek's sinewy torso was so long and mine was so not. My mouth couldn't reach him. I attempted to wiggle away and he held me tighter and spanked my bottom. Oh, God, the first trickle of my juices released. This was impossible. It was like bobbing for apples or in this case a giant cucumber.

I dug my feet into the bed and lurched for his dick. He welded my quivering cunt to his face, and reprimanded me with quick slaps on my ass. I forged to the finish line that I didn't want to cross yet.

I couldn't hold on much longer. "Oh, God! Derek, Derek, I can't get to your... Oh... My... God... You are so not playing fair." My only recourse was to stroke him with my hand. When I did, he fired on all cylinders. One arm fastened me into place, but his other hand was free to drive his nimble fingers inside me. I caved. I couldn't take it anymore.

"You win! Oh, God, I'm going to come."

My sex flooded beneath me. But I wasn't done yet. I fisted the comforter and braced for an obliterating orgasm. Derek doubled his efforts and rocked me to a screaming, pussy-melting climax. He triumphed over my pussy and me, but in the best way possible.

I couldn't move, in my spongy blissful state. Finally, I summoned the strength to hurl myself up and cuddle next to him.

Derek grinned from ear to ear. "Did I hear you say, I win?"

I giggled in my defeat. "Yes, you win, but in a way, I think I did. You're amazing...and a total cheater because I couldn't reach. So, what do you want?"

"You first. If you had won, what would you have wanted?"

"Nothing. I have everything. I have you. You're all I've ever wanted."

He pressed his lips to mine and then I remembered Molly. Where the heck was Molly? She came upstairs with us and was on her doggie bed, but I left our bedroom door open.

I jolted upright. "Where's Molly?"

"She's fine. She stayed on her dog bed."

"I guess she was in here the entire time we were up to no good. We can't ever take her to a pet psychic, she already knows too much."

"I think we're getting off track here. There's a matter of a debt to settle. There is something I'd like you to do for me."

"What?"

He sat up, took my hand and caressed my cheek. "Nia, I know it freaked you out when I wanted to add your name to all of my assets, and I don't want to push, but I do want to add your name to the deed of this house. This is your house too. It's our house. It's our home."

A lump formed in my throat, and a single tear rolled down my cheek. No one had ever been more wonderful to me than my beautiful fiancé.

I looked into his ice-blue eyes beaming with warmth. "Okay, thank you."

Derek cloaked me in his arms, and my love for him

skyrocketed.

He eased me on my back and we made love. The electricity of our powerful connection flashed like a shooting star. He filled me fully and took me slow and easy. I cherished every moment he was inside me. With him, I was home.

* * * *

Derek took Molly out for one last potty. He returned to the bedroom with our puppy tucked under his arm. He was about to put her back on the doggie bed.

"Can she sleep in the bed with us?"

"Okay, you both are so hard to say no to. Eventually she might get too big. We probably shouldn't make it a habit."

She scampered into my arms.

I scratched Molly on the white splash of fur on her chest. "We'll see. I think she likes it up here. She wants to be a part of the pack."

Derek climbed in bed. "I almost forgot. My mom wanted me to tell you she would love to host the wedding at their estate. She's been dying to throw a big, fancy wedding ever since my sister, Dina eloped. Of course, we'd probably need to do it the last weekend of July. August might be too hot for an outdoor wedding, and September I start shooting *First Bite*. If we don't do it then we would have to wait until spring."

My skin flushed and my heart raced. July was too soon. We were still getting to know each other. Plus, I never imagined a big, fancy wedding. What could I say? It was such a generous offer.

"That's so nice of your mom, but I won't have time to plan everything."

"I told her you'd say that and Mom told me to let you know she would take care of everything. The only thing you have to do is get a dress and say I do."

It felt like the walls were closing in on me. "I'll be right back." I flew out of bed and rushed to the bathroom.

"Oh, and don't think I forgot about your swimming lesson. We should do it tomorrow since I'm leaving town. You're going to love it."

I sank down on the tiles in the bathroom. My head dizzied. Am I overreacting? Maybe tomorrow I would feel differently. After all, he had sprung it on me. I should sleep on it. It was the perfect plan.

# Chapter Two

I tossed and turned. My plan to sleep on it was a big, fat failure. I was so mad at myself for reacting this way. I had no right to turn down Derek's mom. It wasn't fair for me to demand a small, intimate wedding, since I already had a big, fancy one.

I pictured this sea of family and friends on Derek's side of the aisle and no family on my side. Of course, Aunt Mary Jane and Uncle Bill would try to come. They were all I had.

My mind drifted back to my wedding with Nick. I thought about his parents. How awful it must have been for them to lose their son. I still had Nick's ring, the Ryan family heirloom. Somehow, I would return it to them.

Derek's words about the swim lesson echoed in my head. How and the hell could I get out of it? I couldn't face it yet. My brain was like a computer with all the tabs opened. I was cold and sweaty. *Oh God, am I having a panic attack?* I jerked up in bed, fighting to catch my breath.

Derek flipped on the light. "Sweetie, are you okay?"

My voice trembled. "I don't think so."

"Come here, just breathe."

I let go a lungful of air.

He rubbed my back. "There, that's, my good girl. I need you to talk to me. Tell me what's wrong."

"I don't want you to be mad at me, but I don't want a big, fancy wedding. Which makes me an asshole, because I've already had a wedding and you haven't."

Derek clasped my hands. "Do you still want to marry me?"

"Yes, of course I do. It's just that… You have your mom and dad, your sister and her family, not to mention all your friends and your parents' friends. I–I don't even have any one to walk me down the aisle. I don't have a mom and dad." My jaw trembled and tears streamed down my face.

Derek held me tight. "I'm sorry, baby, I should've realized. My God, you're shaking. Were you afraid to tell me?"

"I wasn't afraid. I just didn't want to upset anyone."

He smiled, and smoothed my hair. "You want to know a little secret? I didn't want a big, fancy wedding either. I thought every woman wanted a big wedding and my mom was excited about it, so I didn't say anything."

"So a small wedding is okay with you?"

He pressed his lips to my forehead. "Of course, whatever my girl wants."

I exhaled. "I love you."

"I love you too. Do you want me to turn the TV on

so you can fall asleep?"

I cuddled up next to him. "No, you're all I need."

Derek turned off the light and draped his arms around me. "Goodnight, my sweet girl, get some sleep."

* * * *

Yes, Sunday whizzed by. Everything clicked along according to my plan. I kept Derek distracted and busy. He didn't utter a word about my swimming lesson.

Late in the afternoon, Molly and I enjoyed a rigorous game of fetch in the backyard. Her puppy athletic skills impressed me. She ran like the wind.

Derek was in his office upstairs. He said he would join us after he got off the phone with Aaron. A press release about our engagement would drop tomorrow. I secretly hoped a panda at the zoo would give birth to a chimp and steal our thunder.

I threw the ball for Molly. It rolled under the bushes at the back of the property. It was my turn to fetch so we could resume our game. As I set off to retrieve the ball, I heard a splash. I whipped around, and Molly wasn't there. "Molly!"

I sprinted to the pool and screamed for Derek. She was in the deep end. Without thinking, I jumped in to save her. I tried desperately to push off the bottom of the pool, but I couldn't. I sunk like a stone. I flailed, unable to get my bearings. *Oh, God, please let my puppy be all right.* I kicked my legs, and swung my arms to reach the surface. Nothing worked. I couldn't hold my breath anymore. My lungs filled with water. I was fading…

"Come on, Nia, stay with me. Stay with me, baby."

It felt like there was a brick on my chest. Derek rotated me to my side and I coughed up the water in my lungs.

I gasped for breath. "Molly, where's Molly?"

Derek helped me sit up. "She's fine. She's right here." My little, wet, four-month-old dog was perched by my side.

"How did she get out of the pool?"

"Unlike you, Molly can swim. When I got down here she was already out."

"I'm sorry I scared you. I panicked when I saw her in the water. I didn't think."

Derek's jaw clenched. "I thought I was going to lose you. Don't ever do that to me again."

"I promise, I won't."

Derek stood and offered his hand. "Come on let's go get your swimsuit on."

I didn't move. I felt like a disobedient child.

Derek raised his voice. "Nia, I said let's go. I'm teaching you to swim and I'm doing it right now."

I struggled to find the words. The words I had never said to anyone. I opened my mouth to speak, but nothing came out.

"You are unbelievable. Do you have any idea how much I worry about you when I'm out of town? I worry about Larry Wall getting out of prison and coming after you. I worry about Sonya who isn't even in jail. I worry about Nick's family wanting revenge. The one thing you could do for me is learn to swim so I don't have to worry about you drowning, and you won't fucking do it. Well, that's just great. God damn it!"

I closed my eyes and whispered, "I was in the car."

Derek piped back. "What?"

"I was in the car...I was in the car...I was in the car!"

Derek knelt down beside me. "Nia, I don't know what you're talking about. What car?"

Tears tumbled down my cheeks. "When my mom died in the accident. I was in the car. I wanted to go to a pool party and I couldn't swim. My mom was driving me to my first lesson. I was in the car. It was my fault. It was all my fault."

I completely fell apart. All these years I had never told anyone, not any of my therapists, not even Julia. Derek sat down on the ground and encased himself around me. It was as if he loved all the hurt and devastation out of me while I wept.

"I'm so sorry. It wasn't your fault, sweetie. Shhh... it's okay. I'm right here. I'm not letting go."

In some ways, saying the words aloud was a breakthrough. When I was all cried out, Derek picked me up, carried me upstairs and drew me a hot bath.

I was alone in the tub. Molly was lying on the bath mat. Derek stripped off his wet clothes and threw on some shorts.

"Aren't you coming in?"

"In a minute. I'm going to get us some wine."

While that sounded lovely, what Derek said in anger lingered in my mind. He was right. The harsh reality of Larry Wall being released from prison one day, coupled with Nick's family and Sonya overwhelmed us. Being in denial wasn't an option. The sad truth hit me. We had zero control. I couldn't control my emotions either, but maybe opening up was a good thing. I only worried I'd be too much for Derek.

He returned with our wine, handed me a glass, and knelt down next to the tub.

"I thought you said you were getting in the bath with me?"

"I am, sweet girl. First, I'm going to wash your hair. I want you to relax. Let me take care of you."

Derek turned on the spigot and checked the temperature. "Lean your head back, baby. I've got you."

The warm water and Derek's hands were a tranquil paradise. After he rinsed out the shampoo and applied the conditioner, he treated me to a scalp massage, followed by a heavenly shoulder rub.

I placed my hands on top of his. "You're so good to me. I don't feel like I deserve you."

"Nia, please don't say that. Listen, if I wasn't leaving tomorrow, I wouldn't even suggest this, but... I think we need to talk."

I conceded. "You're right, we do."

Once he rinsed out the conditioner, he climbed in the tub with me.

"Would you feel better if I held you while we talked?"

"Yes, please."

I sat with my back to his front. His strong arms curved around me.

I cuddled into him and exhaled. "I'm really sorry I never told you why I couldn't swim. The truth is, I never told anyone. I buried it deep inside because I couldn't face it. Of course, my dad knew. I use to think he stopped loving me, because if I hadn't wanted to go to a pool party, or I learned to swim like everyone else, it wouldn't have happened."

"I'm sorry you've carried it around with you for so long. I can't even fathom how awful that day was for you. Do you want to talk about it?"

I turned and faced him. "Do I have to?"

"No, of course not. I would like you to talk about it with your therapist, Dr. Roma. Can you do that for me?"

"Yes. And I promise I'll learn to swim. You're right. You shouldn't have to worry about me when you're not here, especially when the worry plate is already full."

"I'm always going to do everything I can to protect you. But when I'm not here, I feel like I don't have control."

I laughed a little. "Welcome to my world."

He kissed the top of my wet head. "I love your laugh. I want to you to keep making us laugh until we're old and gray."

It was the perfect opening to ask if I was too much for him, so I took it. "Are you sure you still feel that way?"

He put me on his lap. "Sweetie, how can you even ask me that?"

"Because we've been engaged for only two days and I've had two major meltdowns. Don't you want to run away screaming in the night?"

"Nothing could be further from the truth. If anything I worry you'll run away."

"Derek, I love you so much. Why would you think that?"

"I know you do, and I love you more than anything. But sometimes I worry my life, and this crazy business…I'm afraid it will drive you away from me. Tomorrow the press release is coming out about our engagement. You're going to be in the spotlight even more. It isn't always easy. I wish I wasn't leaving tomorrow. I'm going to miss you and Molly too."

When Molly heard her name, she did her best to place her paws on the edge of the tub. She wasn't very successful, but adorable.

I laughed. "Do you want in the tub? Do you want to get a bath?"

Molly got down, grabbed the bathmat in her mouth,

and took off.

Derek stood and extended his hand. "That is one smart dog."

"Yep, we better get out of here. It's dinnertime. She might eat the bathmat."

He helped me up and drew me into his arms. "Hey, promise me, from now on, when we need to have a talk, you'll let me hold you in the tub."

"I promise."

I dried my hair while Derek fed Molly and ordered pizza. I planned to make spicy shrimp and avocado salad, but we were as hungry as Molly. He got the only takeout I would eat, Grimaldi's pizza with red peppers and mushrooms.

It wasn't very late, but Derek insisted on putting me to bed.

I climbed in bed, but wasn't happy about it. "Are you sure you don't have a little time for your horny fiancée?"

He tucked me in. "Young lady, I don't think you realize how tired you are. Just trust me, and close your eyes." I grabbed for the remote to turn on the TV. Derek snatched it. "No. No TV. You need sleep."

"Okay, but you are so missing out. I wanted to do more butt stuff."

Derek laughed. "Butt stuff? I think butt stuff can wait. Close your eyes for me. I'll be right here until you fall asleep."

I hated to admit it, but he was right. I was out like a

light.

When I woke, Derek was in bed with me. I was wide-awake. "Hey, what time is it?"

"It's after midnight. You've been out for almost four hours. Do you want to go back to sleep?"

I was refreshed and the heaviness of the day had disappeared. "No way, your fiancée is still horny." Then I remembered my joke from earlier. "I was just kidding about the butt stuff."

Derek arched his eyebrow and grinned. "Really, is that so?"

"I mean, I kind of like, you know, that one thing, but something else is way too big. I don't think it would ever…fit.

"Baby, I didn't come in here for butt stuff. I just want you."

He gave me that look and we were lost in one another. He took his time with me in his own gentle, tender way. It was as if every sweet kiss and soft touch melted away the pain from my past. We flowed together like a glorious symphony of passion and absolute devotion. We were one body, one soul, one heart, entwined in love.

# Chapter Three

"Nia, your new student is here for their private spin," Shannon said in her upbeat yet professional tone.

"Thanks, I'll be right in."

I must say, I loved being coordinator at the Country Club. I had awesome support staff. Shannon Taylor was much more outgoing and friendly than Sonya. Plus, she respected me, even though she was older than I was. The same was true for my assistant, Lacey Wilson. They both possessed great energies and genuinely enjoyed their jobs.

These days, I had more requests for private classes than I could manage. I usually did five privates a week.

Sometimes new members requested me because they wanted to meet Derek Pierce's girlfriend. What would happen once our engagement news broke?

I trekked to the group exercise room to meet my new student. I was surprised to find him on his bike warming up. I wasn't late. In fact, I was ten minutes early. How odd, he opened up the equipment closet and helped himself to a bike. He appeared to be in his early forties and in decent shape, over six feet, with graying hair.

I offered my hand. "Hi, I'm Nia Kelly."

Before I could say another word, he interrupted. "I

know who you are. I requested you. I'm Walter. Walter James."

"Nice to meet you, Mr. James."

I could've called him Walter. The club wasn't nearly as formal as it used to be, but Walter put out a strange vibe. It was even more bizarre that he requested me, since his manner was so aloof.

What a long, wacky hour! When he asked if I was available the next day for another private, I declined, since I was booked. I palmed him off on Lacey. I'd probably have to pay her double.

After class, I ran home to shower, pick up Molly, and slide my beautiful engagement ring on my finger. I was afraid to wear it while I worked out. I was worried something would happen to it.

It would be a big debut, showing off my ring and Molly. I was beyond excited to share our news.

Before Derek left this morning, he made me promise not to *Google* us, or get online and hunt for news about the engagement. In order to keep our lives private and protect us from the "haters," we steered clear of social media.

I had Molly on a leash and we strode into the club. Shannon, Lacey, Sue Peterson, and the chorus girls, Nancy and Sharon huddled at the front desk. As soon as we walked in, they swarmed me in jubilation.

Sue couldn't contain herself. "Nia, is it true? Are you engaged?"

With a giddy smile, I showed them my left hand.

"Yep, Derek and I are getting married!" A bevy of hugs and cheers ensued.

Lacey high-fived me. "Wow, man, he is so hot. Does he have a brother?"

They gathered around, took a gander at my ring and greeted little fifteen-pound Molly. She was quite the social butterfly. I was proud of her.

"By the way, how did you know we were engaged? Did Brooke tell you?"

Shannon showed me her computer. "No, it's all over the Internet."

I wasn't supposed to look, but I did anyway. Displayed on her screen was an entertainment magazine. There was a nice picture of Derek and me from the *First Bite* premiere. I read the little blurb and made the mistake of scrolling down to the comment section. I only read the first five and they were all negative. One said if he was marrying me, he must be gay and I was his beard. The others commented I wasn't good enough or pretty enough for him. My God, I already felt that way. Did I really have to read it in print? People could be so cruel. Shannon was the only one who saw and she quickly clicked off the site.

A lump formed in my throat. "Thanks for all the well-wishes, but, I better get back to work. I need to submit payroll before the end of the day."

I trudged to my office with Molly and locked myself away.

Ten minutes later, Shannon knocked on the door.

"Hey, I hope you aren't taking any of those stupid comments to heart?"

"It's kind of hard not to. I should've listened to Derek and stayed off the Internet."

"Unfortunately we live in the world of technology where any moron can say whatever idiotic thing that pops into their tiny brain. People are just jealous. To be honest, if I didn't know you, I'd be jealous too. Don't get me wrong, I'm so happy for you, but it's hard to be divorced and single in Vegas. Lacey always says, all the good ones are taken and the rest are *toats* crazy."

Shannon was right. I found the love of my life. She deserved that too, and had so much to offer. She was smart and funny with blonde hair and hazel eyes. Shannon was the whole package.

"Thank you, I needed to hear that. You know, the perfect person for you is out there too. You're a catch."

She headed to the door, responding in her dry humor, "Why thank you. In the meantime, if you need me I will be online stalking Ryan Gosling."

After work, Molly and I returned home. I planned to pop in and say hi to Julia, Phillip, and the dogs, but she said they were busy. I didn't have a chance to talk to her or Brooke all weekend. I was in serious need of some girl time with my two best friends. I picked up the phone to call Steve and Scott. Before I hit send, the doorbell rang.

"Hey, guys, we must have ESP, I was calling you. Come on in."

They weren't their normal lighthearted selves. Steve was especially down.

We sat in the kitchen. "Is everything all right?" I asked.

"Well, we have some bad news." Steve said. "My dad in Buffalo has lung cancer."

"Oh, my God, I'm so sorry. I had no idea."

"Thanks. Scott and I have been talking, and well, were moving back east to take care of him."

"When are you moving?"

Steve looked to Scott to respond. "We're moving in a week."

"A week? Wow, I'm really going to miss you."

"This is something we've been working on for a while," Steve explained. "We just didn't want to say anything unless it was definite. We were going to tell you the other night at the barbeque, but you just got engaged, and we didn't want to spoil the party."

When I first came to town, Steve and Scott welcomed me with open arms. At our TV binge watching parties they kept my wineglass full and laughed at all my jokes. What more could a girl want? They also helped me build my spin classes at the club. They were the ones who told the Peterson's and chorus girls about me.

I asked, "What about your house?"

"We've decided to sell the house," Steve replied. "We already have jobs lined up in Buffalo. I'm afraid the move is permanent."

Scott added, "There's a new member at the club, Walter James. He's our real estate agent."

"I met him today. I think he's kind of strange."

Steve nodded in agreement. "Kind of? I told Scott I didn't think he could sell a rainbow flag at a gay pride parade."

Scott bristled. "I know, but he lives close by and he just got his Nevada license. He's very anxious to establish himself. I'm sure it'll be fine. I'm sorry to spring this on you and go, but we have a ton of packing to do."

"I understand. Do you think we could have one last get-together with the gang? Does Saturday work?"

For the first time, Steve smiled. "Yeah, Saturday works. And don't make a fuss, just something small and quaint."

As I walked them to the door I asked, "You guys are still going to come to the wedding?"

Scott chimed in. "We wouldn't miss it."

"Good, I need someone to throw the bouquet to. Just think, now you two could get married in Nevada and New York."

Steve giggled and Scott shot me a death glare. Well, leave it to me, I opened up my giant mouth and started trouble. Yep, that seemed just about right.

I was so relieved when my phone rang. It was Derek. After the weird class with Walter James, the mean comments about us online, and hearing Steve and Scott news, I needed to hear his calm voice. As usual,

Derek soothed all my anxieties.

When we hung up he said, "Goodnight my beautiful, sweet girl. I love you."

# Chapter Four

My God! Did I have the plague? I texted Brooke, Julia, Lacey, and Shannon, but I didn't hear a peep from anyone. Where was everybody? I even considered texting Sue Peterson, but then I remembered she didn't text. She was not a fan of technology and still used a dinosaur flip phone. I called it a "Cell-a-sauras." This sucked. Molly and I were a little lonely without Derek.

It was early evening when I finally got a text from Julia. "Sorry I've been so busy. Can you come over tonight? Bring Molly. She can play with Coco and Sammy."

Well good, at least I heard from Julia. I texted her back and let her know I'd be there in a half hour.

Julia opened the door, sporting a huge, suspicious grin. What was she up to? Once we landed in the kitchen, the girls shouted, "Surprise!"

Lacey, Shannon, Sue, Brooke, Nancy, and Sharon were in Julia's TV room, surrounded by decorations of assorted penises!

I asked, "What in cock's name is going on?"

They all laughed and Julia said, "It's your bridal shower. I was worried you and Derek would run off and get married and I wouldn't get a chance to give you a proper send off."

"And by proper, you mean penises."

"Actually they were Lacey's idea."

Lacey raised a glass. "I figured if we were going do it, it might as well be fun. Anyone can give you sheets. Keeping things hot between the sheets is more important."

God I loved Lacey. I hadn't known her very long, but she was one of the coolest people I'd ever met, so carefree, with a vibrancy that was contagious. She was quite an athlete too. She played basketball in college and was six feet tall in heels.

I was lucky to be in this unique circle of women. We were all different ages and backgrounds, but the more we hung out, the more fun we had.

Julia refreshed the cocktails and we loosened up. Naturally, the subject went right to sex. It was the perfect cue for me to open my gifts. There was a theme to all my presents—sexy lingerie with a naughty toy.

"When did you guys do all this?"

Nancy said, "We decorated last night, and made a field trip to the mall and the Adult Superstore this afternoon."

No wonder I couldn't get a hold of anyone. I would've loved to be a fly on the wall at the dirty store. I just couldn't picture Sue, Nancy, and Sharon at one of those places. Boy was I wrong. Their gifts were the filthiest, especially Sue's. I sat there speechless with my new garters and stocking ensemble and this thing. It was black and the slightest bit pliable. If you turned it to the side, it sort of looked like a large gold fish with a loop for a tail.

Sue said in a matter-of-fact tone, "That is a butt plug, and it is marvelous."

We howled with laughter. I needed another cocktail after that. I flew to the kitchen to retrieve my libation and when I returned, the girls discussed anal sex as if they were exchanging recipes. Did everyone do butt stuff, but me? When did that get on the menu?

Even more shocking, Shannon shared, "My ex used to like it when I put my finger in his ass hole right before he came."

Jesus, Mary, and Joseph! I had no idea my gal pals were so kinky. All the ladies except Brooke and I nodded in agreement.

I continued opening up my gifts—a dominatrix outfit and riding crop from Sharon, handcuffs, a blindfold, and a red, silk negligée from Nancy, vibrating panties with remote control and matching bra from Julia. Shannon presented me with an assortment of crotchless panties and what I assumed were nipple clamps. *Yikes!* The little black, lacy two-piece outfit from Lacey was sexy, but the toy was a bit of a question mark. It was in the shape of an egg and had a remote too. She explained it went inside me and vibrated like my panties. My instructions were to give both remotes to Derek.

That was when I noticed the other theme at play. "You guys realize your gifts require me to give up all control. Are you trying to tell me something?"

They all chimed in sarcastically, "No never. Would we do that?"

Brooke responded, "Well, not all of them." Of course, my fellow "no butt stuff" sister had my back. Her gift was my favorite. A silky black robe with a gorgeous bustie' and matching thong. The toy was a small, feather tickler. She also gave me massage oil and lotions. "Thank you all so much. I'm sure Derek will thank you too."

The room grew quiet, while the girls exchanged shifty glances.

Sue took the bull by horns. "Nia, we've all been very forthcoming about our sex lives and you haven't said a word."

"Yeah, spill it. I bet Derek is amazing in bed. Am I right?" Sharon asked.

I actually blushed. I didn't talk about those things. Derek and I were so guarded and private. For once, I was relieved to hear my cell phone ringing. I sprang to the kitchen to answer it.

It was Derek. "Hi, sweetie. How's my girl?"

"I'm great. Julia threw me a surprise bridal shower. Wait until you see my presents. They're actually for you."

The girls weren't letting me off the hook, even if I was on the phone. They hollered, "Hey, we want details. You've got to give us something."

"Nia, what's going on?"

"The girls want me to divulge one of our dirty little sex secrets."

"Oh, do they? It's probably not a good idea."

"I've got to give them something." I declared to the girls, "Derek says my lips are like pillows, all of them."

They laughed and Julia taunted, "Ah, come on, you can do better than that."

Hearing the exchanges Derek teased. "Tell those ladies to leave my girl alone."

"Derek says to tell the ladies to leave me alone."

Lacey joked. "If I see a lady, I'll tell her."

We all cracked up. Before I hung up Derek told me he loved me and missed me. And I should be getting a package from him tomorrow. How exciting.

When I said goodnight to the girls, I invited everyone to our house Saturday night for Steve and Scott's going away party. Per Steve and Scott's request, it was turning into a circus. In less than twenty-four hours, the guest list grew by leaps and bounds. So much for not making a fuss, I was happy to host the big top. It would be an evening we'd never forget.

* * * *

Molly and I were snuggled in bed. I was about to turn out the light when I got a text from Derek. "Goodnight, my sweet girl, I can't wait to marry you."

I fell right to sleep.

* * * *

Just what was in my mystery package from Derek? As I opened the box, Molly waited patiently. What a smart dog, Derek sent her a toy. It was a purple and orange squeaking platypus. I gave it to her and she shook it like a rag doll. Next, I found a bottle of lavender lotion. How sweet. I mentioned I wanted some to help me sleep.

The rest of the items were a gentle reminder. There were water wings, an inner tube, nose pinchers, an old school white swim cap, and a light grey swimsuit that looked like it belonged in the museum of hideous and frumpy. Derek was a man with a plan, but why the *frump-tastic* swimsuit? I had plenty of bikinis. I texted him, "I got your package. May I ask what you're up to?"

He texted back, "I cannot risk being distracted by your hot little ass or any of your other heavenly body parts when I teach you to swim. You will have to follow my rules, dear student."

I texted, "My teacher is so hard."

Derek didn't miss a beat. "Not right now, but I will be if you wear a bikini. BTW, did Molly like her toy?"

Before I could answer, Molly dragged her platypus out the doggie door. The same person who put in Julia's came this morning to install it.

When I got outside I couldn't find Molly right away and it scared me. I screamed for her as I searched the backyard. I heard a bark, turned around and there was Sammy. "Hey, buddy, how did you get out?" He barked again and scampered to the bushes at the back of property. I followed him, and sure enough, there was Molly, and a stockpile of her favorite toys.

"Come here, my little weirdo. What's with the stash of toys?"

As Molly crawled out Sammy gave her a little what for. It was as if Sammy said, "Don't run off like that and frighten your mom again." We went back to the house and I called Julia to let her know Sammy was with me. I asked her if he could spend the night.

Julia and Phillip were in full baby making mode and not traveling as much. I didn't dog sit Sammy and Coco like I used to. Of course, she said yes, and asked if she should send Coco over too. We laughed because Miss Coco loved Julia's undivided attention.

I quickly texted Derek to tell him what transpired. Then the dogs and I hurried out for a play.

When we came inside there was another text from Derek. "I'm going to bed, baby. I hope the lotion helps you sleep. I can't wait to see you on Friday. PS I will be tending to your greedy pussy all weekend. Please have it ready for me. I'm planning on taking you, hard and often."

*Holy shit!* My fiancé *sexted* me. He was probably sleeping, so I couldn't text back that I was getting a Brazilian wax tomorrow. Damn it. His text made me horny. Derek still insisted I save all my pleasure for him. Tonight would be a challenge.

Sammy, Molly, and I snuggled up in bed. I channel surfed, searching for something disgusting to watch. It would surely take my mind off Derek's text. There it was…*Hoarders*. Nothing could destroy my lady boner faster than an unorganized house in the throws of chaos. Between my lavender lotion and the piles of newspapers and Beanie Babies on TV, my eyes grew heavy. Before I drifted off, I had a realization. Molly had a secret pile of toys in the yard. Perhaps we had a little hoarder on our hands?

# Chapter Five

I quaked in my heels while anxiously waiting for Derek in the upstairs hallway. As per instructions, I wore one of my new outfits with my freshly waxed pussy.

My God, since the first sexy text, I'd been in sheer agony anticipating the feel of Derek's hands on me. Thursday night he was ruthless, describing in explicit detail every way he wanted to take me this weekend. When I texted him I was so horny I'd have to tend to myself, he said if I did, he'd spank me until my bottom glowed. That just turned me on more. In my efforts to be good, I did all my homework for my online Statistics 2 course, but made the mistake of rereading his text messages right before bed. I totally caved. It did nothing to quell the aching need between my legs. I was a bad girl who craved her punishment.

I paced in the hallway and caught a glimpse of myself in the mirror. I loved the feel of the silky, black robe against my skin. *Well, fuck.* I was almost sexy. I ran my fingers over the bustie.' It was like magic. It nearly gave me a cleavage. My hands floated over my waist, toward my sex. Do I dare?

"Nia, I'm home."

I jumped and composed myself.

Every cell in my body sizzled as his footsteps bounded up the stairs.

He stood before me with desire flaring in his eyes. The air radiated with our smoldering connection. It was an indescribable, mind-blowing force of nature. With just one look, we were lost in each other, lost to one another.

My pulse spiked as Derek's gaze drank me in. "You look fucking amazing. Come here."

Wobbly legs carried me to him and he fused our bodies together. I offered him my mouth and he took it —hard. Our needy murmurs and moans echoed in the hallway. The ache between my legs grew to an anguishing, wet throb.

He backed me into the wall. "Turn around."

I faced the wall. He slipped off my silk robe and tossed it aside. His arms snaked around my waist and clutched me to him. He brushed my hair to one side, leaving my neck free for the taking. His fingertips ran along the curve followed by his lips. He inhaled. "Your scent makes me crazy. I can't wait to be inside you. I bet there's a greedy pussy waiting for me."

His hand dove between my legs and discovered my saturated thong. "Your panties are wet."

I pleaded. "Rip them off, please."

Derek shredded them from my body, and dipped a finger inside my trembling need.

He whispered roughly. "Were you a good girl? Did you save all your pleasure for me?

I succumbed to this thrusting finger and ignored his daunting query. "Oh, God, ah…ah, it feels so good."

"Answer the question. And don't lie to me." He toyed and teased me with his hand. I didn't want him to stop.

"I…ah fuck…I was a bad girl."

His hand retreated and he spun me around. His eyes still blazed with lust, but a hint of playfulness danced on the corners of his mouth. "What did I say would happen if you pleasured yourself?"

I swallowed hard. "You would spank me."

"And you did it anyway?"

I sucked my finger in my mouth and circled it on my wanton clit. "I did."

Derek shook his head. "You're so fucking bad." With masterful agility, he tore off my bustie', leaving me naked in heels. "Go ahead, turn around. You're going to be punished."

I did what he said, accepting my decadent fate. My palms flattened against the wall, I could hear the thud of my heartbeat.

What was happening? He wasn't spanking me. His clothes hit the floor and then it grew quiet. I protruded my ass, yearning to feel the sharp, crack of his hand.

Finally, his fingers peeled back my outer lips. Maybe he was going to spank my pussy. I panted, craving more. Once again, his hand retreated. The length of his steely cock rubbed along my wet slit, taunting me. An influx of my juices dribbled on his flirty fuck stick. He was playing with me. That was my real punishment. If it was another race to the finish line, I'd bet it all on me.

His hands perched on my hips as if he was waiting for the gunshot. His tip rested at my opening and plowed inside. I cried out at its rough entry. Derek was unabashed in his searing thrusts. My body zinged and zagged with his and longed for release. He was slaying my mischievous cunt with grueling force. My hands slipped. Derek caught me around the waist and slowed.

He coiled my hair around his hand and pulled me to him. "When I do spank your ass, it will be bright red if you come."

He led me to the floor. I was on my hands and knees ready to receive the rest of my chastening. His hand flew to my engorged clit. There was no way I couldn't come. A red ass was in my future. *Hell yes! Bring it on!*

His hands gripped my hips as he resumed his raging strokes. They awakened the sucking power of my tight hole. He fucked me to an abyss of incoherent shrieks. His myriad of unrestrained thrusts took me to unimaginable heights.

"Are you going to come for me and earn that red ass?"

A vigorous spasm rocked my inner walls and I came unhinged. "Ah, I'm coming. I'm so fucking coming."

Derek's vast, warm release fractured inside me and

reduced us to a breathless mass of jelly on the floor.

He cradled my wrung-out sweaty body to his. "My angel, you were fantastic."

"I'm no angel. I was bad, twice. Are you going to spank me now?"

He cupped my face. "You're always so eager, but no. Right now, I want to hold you in the tub. Come."

* * * *

We were in the tub, my back to his front. Derek surrounded me in his limbs. We were quiet while we recovered from our playtime.

Then Derek said, "I still feel terrible about the comments you read on the Internet. I'm going to do everything I can to keep our lives as private as possible."

"I know you will. It just took me by surprise. But, I did what you said and I've been staying off the computer as much as possible."

He pressed his lips to my temple. "That's my good girl. I do need to talk to you about something." I sat up and he nestled me back into place. "Don't worry. It's nothing bad, I promise. I talked to my mom and she completely understood about the wedding. After she thought about it, a small intimate wedding made more sense. But she was wondering if it would be okay to throw us an engagement party at their estate."

I let the request sink in. It actually sounded like

fun, on one condition. "Sure, that's so nice. I just have one request."

"Anything, sweetie. What's your request?"

I turned to him. "No gifts. We don't need fancy china or twenty toasters. Instead of gifts, our guests could make a donation to Sammy's Place."

The charity I started with Sara from the humane center and Karen from the women's shelter needed more room. Sadly, we were almost at capacity all the time. I could put myself on display and give up a little privacy if that meant more women, children, and their pets had a safe place to stay, away from their abusers.

Derek cupped my chin and smiled. "That sounds perfect, just like you."

* * * *

"Wow, I think I'm speechless," Derek exclaimed as he surveyed the gifts from my surprise bridal shower.

I hid all the outfits, so when I wore them he would be surprised, but the toys were a different story. I spread them out on the kitchen table, after dinner.

He picked up the butt plug, with a gleam in his eyes. "Hmm…interesting."

"I actually didn't know what that was for, but now I do."

"How do you feel about it?"

"Well, I feel that almost everyone is getting it up the ass except for me. Is that really what all men want?"

Derek took a moment to contemplate his answer. He responded in a comical matter-of-fact tone, "Yes, yes we do. Men are pigs. All men think about it all the time. And if they say they don't they're lying."

I burst out laughing. "Have you ever…done… that?"

"No, I haven't."

"But you think about it all time?"

Derek ran his fingers through his hair, sat on one of the kitchen chairs and pulled me onto his lap. "Come here. Of course, I've thought about it, but I would never expect you to do that unless you wanted to. Have you ever?"

This conversation sent a wave of heat through my body. I licked my lips. "I haven't ever done it, or even wanted to. That is, until now. I mean, maybe." The idea that we could be each other's first was very alluring.

"You know we have the rest of our lives to explore each other. I'm looking forward to playing and experiencing all kinds of new pleasures with you. Lucky for us, your friends gave us a starter kit."

Derek was perfection. He was the ultimate blend of sweet and sexy.

I peered into his gorgeous ice-blue eyes. "Where should we begin?"

He picked up the black lace vibrating panties. "I think we should start with these. You should wear them tomorrow night at Steve and Scott's going away party." He pointed to the remote. "But I'm taking this. I'll be the one in control."

I fingered the butt plug. "Can we play with that next?"

He grinned in that devilish way. "Only if you insist."

"Yes, I insist."

He rested his forehead on mine. "And when it comes to anything else, it's your decision. You have to be ready."

"Does lube come by the gallons?"

We snickered and I threw my arms around his neck. He held me close while our laughter subsided. When he released me, I glanced to his crotch. I wasn't the only one turned on by our conversation. Derek's erection wanted to break free from his shorts.

I stood up and stripped out of my clothes. "So, what are you thinking about right now?"

"Sordid fuck filth."

Derek followed suit and got naked. His long, herculean body settled back down on the kitchen chair. Our eyes locked on one another in an erotic daze. He patted his lap.

I broke out in goose flesh. "Is it time for my spanking?"

"No. I'm not going to take you over my knee. You're going to fuck us into oblivion. Come here.

*Hell yeah, I was!*

Just a single glance at Derek's rippled physique, immersed me in wetness. Everything about him made me burn, his broad shoulders, his brawny rock-solid body, his sexy jawline, and those eyes. One look—my look—evaporated me and sent a shock through me all at once.

I straddled his lap. "Are you ready for oblivion?"

"Absolutely." He brought two fingers to my mouth. "Suck."

My mouth took them inside. I caressed them as if I was sucking his cock.

A low groan rattled in Derek's throat. "Hmm... superb." He removed his fingers and fondled them over my lush, satiny folds. "Feel that, always so ready for me."

He drew his lips to mine and devoured me with sweeping strokes of his tongue. Audible whimpers and carnal moans peppered the air. His hands cupped my ass cheeks and steered me to the head his of concrete shaft. I slowly shunted myself, taking all of him inside my slippery tunnel. He was buried inside me fully, our bodies interlaced like sinful vines. I leaned back, placed my hands on his thighs, churning and circling my hips.

Derek growled. "That's it. Work my cock. Yes." His fingers treated my naughty nub to the irresistible friction it craved. I shifted my grinding hips into high gear, forging a frothy drizzle between my thighs. My pussy bubbled around him as I gorged myself on his thick girth. It was so phenomenal. I nearly fell off the chair.

Derek grasped my arms. "That's, my good girl.

Now, put your hands on the back of the chair." His steely-blue eyes bore into me. "My angel, take us to oblivion."

I grabbed on and pumped him with vigor. Derek splayed his hands on my back and released groans of praise for my pumping power. A massive swell of pressure built as he smacked my hot spot. My sobbing cunt drew him inside even further than I thought possible. A surge of white-hot passion ripped through my body. My first orgasm hit me like a tidal wave crashing against my walls. A tremendous rush of liquid escaped, but that was only the beginning.

I thrashed up and down on Derek like a wild animal, bathing him in my climatic juices.

His grip on me tightened. "That's it, baby, just come."

I fucked us to oblivion and beyond. I cranked on him full power and my supercharged pussy sprayed Derek's cock with a never-ending stream.

When his release blew, he clutched me to him and we rode it out together.

Oblivion was fucking awesome! Our wilted, satisfied bodies sealed together and we breathed as one.

Derek's fingertips grazed my back. "Sweetie, you're incredible. When you come like that it feels amazing."

I peeked up at him. "Well, duh." Then I looked at the wet floor. "Oh no."

"What is it, are you okay?"

I put my hands over my face. "I'm fine, it's the floor."

He glanced down. "Very impressive, young lady. There's enough cum on the floor to sink the Titanic. You know, when you texted that Molly was spending the night with Brooke, at first I was bummed since I missed her too. Now I think you made the right call." He lifted me off him and put me on dry land. "Go get ready for bed, sweetie. I'll take care of this."

"Let me help you."

He patted my bottom. "I insist."

* * * *

My heavily sated state brought on exhaustion. I could barely keep my eyes open, but I still hadn't fessed up to the party plans for Steve and Scott.

He climbed in bed, and drew me close. "So, do you think I'll have time to teach you to swim before the party tomorrow night?"

"I don't think so. The party plans have changed a little. Now everyone is coming at four o'clock. And I do mean everyone." *Yikes!* The change could go over like a lead balloon, a lead balloon with a side of rotten hoagies. Derek cocked his head in a charming inquisitive way.

I let out a big sigh. "Okay, this is what happened. Our small intimate party snowballed into a bigger party. Steve wanted to invite friends from work, I said sure, and then Scott asked if he could, and I said why not, the more the merrier. The next thing you know, people from their work asked if they could bring their kids, and then Steve suggested it should be like a carnival with a bouncy house, a snow cone machine, and a stilt walker. I'm sorry. I didn't know what to do. They have so many friends and so little time to say goodbye to everyone."

Derek paused for a moment. It was hard to read him. If he'd sprung this on me, it would've gone over like a lead balloon with a side of crazy sauce.

"You really are like Ado Annie in *Oklahoma*. You know, the girl who can't say no."

"I know, and I should've given you a heads-up, but it all happened so fast. Steve and Scott seemed so excited. Those two could have a second career as event planners. They're so good at it. We don't have to do a thing. They hired a lifeguard, DJ, and got food trucks. The only thing we're doing is supplying the booze, a bartender, and the wait staff. Don't worry I got a recommendation from Marcus, your chef. I made sure they are sending men and no women. I know you don't like women working for you. I just don't know why."

"Like I said, it's just less complicated that way. It's not a big deal."

"Steve and Scott hired a guy to be the lifeguard. A twenty something beefed-up dude named, Bruce. Steve made Bruce his screen saver."

"As long as there are no clowns, I'm good. I've hated clowns since I saw that movie *Poltergeist*."

"Oh shit, I forgot about the clown."

"Nia, please be kidding."

"I wish I was. I hate them too. Brace yourself, because tomorrow Corky the Clown will be in our backyard with his big fucking shoes and stupid ass red nose."

Derek cracked up. "At least there aren't any mimes. For some reason I can't stand them either."

"Oh, my God, me neither. I secretly want to punch them. We get it, you're in a box."

My lame imitation of a mime nearly threw Derek into fits of hysteria. I hurled myself at him in glee. "I love you. Thank you for not being angry with me."

He wrapped his arms around me. "Of course I'm not. I know how much you're going to miss Steve and Scott. I'm going to miss them too. They're sacrificing a lot to go take care of Steve's dad. I'm glad they're getting a big send-off." Derek kissed me softly on the lips and continued in a devilish tone, "Plus, tomorrow night someone promised they're going to wear vibrating panties while I have the remote."

"Okay, but only if you promise not to share the remote with Corky the dumbass Clown. He might try to juggle it with a chain saw and a bologna sandwich.

Derek laughed and turned out the light. "I promise. Now get some sleep, baby. We have a big day tomorrow."

I snuggled up to Derek in my usual spot. I couldn't resist saying one more thing in jest. "Did you hear the one about the magician, the mime, and the juggler?"

He kissed my forehead. "Close your eyes, my sweet girl. I love you."

# Chapter Six

"Did you forget something?" With a dirty twinkle in his eyes, Derek dangled my vibrating panties from his index finger. I hadn't seen him this delighted since he found Buzz hiding in my nightstand.

I sauntered over to him in my naked state. "You weren't really serious about that, were you? I'll be a mess at the party. I won't have any—"

"Control? I think that's the idea. Allow me, I insist." He shimmied my panties up my legs and gave me a little jolt with the remote.

"Oh, my God, Derek, this is going to be my undoing. Be sure to thank Julia. The vibrating panties are from her."

Derek went to his desk and produced several fancy envelopes. "I already did. In fact, I wrote a thank-you note to all the girls."

I was so touched. He always embraced my friends with open arms. How did I get so lucky? I had such mixed emotions about the evening. I would miss Steve and Scott terribly. But I was excited to throw our first party as an engaged couple.

The house hummed all day. We opened up the side gate and Steve and Scott took over. They ushered in assorted vendors for their carnival-themed event. The food trucks parked out on the street, but the snow cone and cotton candy machines were by the bouncy house.

On the other side of the yard, closer to the patio we set up an ample bar. Steve and Scott even got a deluxe "John" so the guests didn't wander through our house. I really appreciated that no one had access but Derek and me.

After an early morning run with Molly, we dropped her off to hang out with Coco and Sammy at Julia's house. With the gate open and all the commotion, it was the safest option.

Before we left the bedroom, Derek put the remote for my vibrating panties in his shorts pocket. "So, my little control freak, with all the great food trucks outside are you going to live dangerously and try something new?"

"I don't think so. I made a berry salad with chicken and kale."

"I guess we should've ordered Grimaldi's."

I elbowed him for teasing me about my food issues. "Am I that bad?"

"No, you're perfect. I love everything you make. In fact, since we've been together the makeup artists have commented that my skin looks great."

"Wow! Not too shabby for an old guy."

He grimaced and closed the distance between us. "Hmm…that reminds me, I owe someone a spanking. You've just added a few swats. Your bottom is going to be fire-engine red."

I floated my arms around his neck. "Bring it on, Mr. Pierce."

"Oh, I intend to, Miss Kelly."

* * * *

Derek and I stepped out onto the patio and took in the view. Steve and Scott positioned everything in its perfect place. It was going to be quite a party. The guests arrived along with the DJ, Bruce the lifeguard, Corky the Clown, and Tiffany the stilt walker. I wasn't thrilled the stilt walker was a woman. She ignored the children and sidled up to the men. Plus, her outfit wasn't very kid friendly. Her princess's boobs spilled out of her top. She looked like Sleeping Beauty's slutty sister, and nearly fell off her stilts when she spotted my fiancé.

I rolled my eyes at Derek and he laughed. He excused himself when he saw my gal pals huddled together, except for Shannon and Lacey. He took off to deliver their thank-you notes. While he did that, I checked-in with the guests of honor.

I watched Derek out of the corner of my eye. He was such a charmer as he delivered each note, whispering in their ear and chuckling.

Steve, Scott, and I joined them, followed by Phillip, Tom, and Jeff. It hit me this would be the last time we were all together like this. It was sad.

Sue was emotional too. "I'm going to miss you

guys so much. It really hasn't sunk in yet. I mean, if it weren't for Steve and Scott we never would've gone to spin class and met all of you."

Jeff slung his arm around Sue's shoulder. "Sue's right. Not to mention my little tiger here is in the best shape of her life." He tickled her playfully.

She giggled. "Jeff, stop."

"I speak the truth," Jeff said as slid his arm around her waist.

Jeff and Sue were in amazing shape and still hot for each other. If I were a doctor, I would prescribe orgasms and exercise for everyone.

Tom piped up rather sheepishly, "At the risk of getting all of the guys in trouble, can we just take a moment and check out the stilt walker?"

Brooke playfully socked him in the arm. "Tom!"

"Sweetheart, what I mean is, I don't understand how she remains upright. Ten to one she face-plants before the end of the night."

Phillip chimed in, "Oh please, let it be on me!"

Julia added, "Well, at least she'll have two large flotation devices to break her fall."

While everyone chuckled, Derek hit the vibrating panty remote. It jolted me and I let out a whoop after everyone else quieted down. I shot him a look and he was quite pleased with himself.

Earlier he warned me not to go out of remote range, which was about twenty-five feet. If I did, I would be punished accordingly. My ass and I craved its discipline and we were bad on purpose. I grabbed Julia's hand and we moseyed to the bar. In this heat, the crisp white wine went down fast and easy.

The bar was right outside the vibrating panty range. When I turned to face Derek, he reached in his pocket and hit the remote and nothing happened. I smiled and shrugged my shoulders. He shook his head and grinned.

I poured myself another large refill. "I'm in absolute agony, Julia Dixon, and it's your fault."

"What did I do?"

"Derek made me wear your bridal shower gift. I've been vibrating all night."

We laughed and slugged back a refreshing gulp. She grabbed my hand. "Nia, Derek loves you so much. Whatever happens remember that."

"I know he loves me…I… Why are you being so serious?"

"Hey, look Shannon and Lacey are here. Let's go say hi." Julia bopped off in their direction.

I followed behind her and Derek joined us. He gave them their thank-you notes and whispered something in their ears. Maybe I was being paranoid, but after what Julia said, was something odd going on?

Speaking of odd, Walter James appeared on the patio. I didn't want to invite him to the party, but we invited the entire street, so no one would complain about the noise and the food trucks. I ran into him on one of my walks with Molly. Seeing him leave Larry Wall's old house was unsettling. I passed by their house a lot since it was halfway between our house and Julia's. It was a constant reminder Larry Wall would get out of jail one day.

As Walter approached our group, my stomach churned.

Lacey blurted out a little too loudly, "Oh man, who invited Walter the Weird? That guy gives me the creeps. Please tell me he isn't the only single dude here."

Shannon interjected. "Lacey, he'll hear you. Plus, I don't think he's that bad."

"That's because you don't have to spend an hour alone with him in a private spin class. Julia, please point me in the direction of the bar."

Julia took Lacey by the hand and escorted her to the bar. Shannon beamed and waved at Walter. Perhaps she had a little crush on him. If he was okay with Shannon, I should give him a chance.

I extended my hand. "Hey, Walter, you made it. This is my fiancé Derek Pierce."

The two men exchanged a firm handshake. Walter said, "Nice to meet you. Oh, and congratulations on your engagement. It's a shame the tabloids are giving you two such a rough time. Just so you know, I don't believe a word of it."

There was a moment of silence, and awkwardness filled the air. Derek didn't say a word.

Shannon intervened. "Nia, Walter must be talking about those comments you saw on Monday.

Remember? It was just a bunch of idiots."

"Yeah, sorry. That's what I meant."

I stared at the ground wondering if I should ask Derek about what Walter said. Before I could, a little girl tugged on his shorts. She had dark wavy hair and big brown eyes.

"Excuse me, Mister? Are you the guy on that show?"

Derek knelt down so he could be at eye level with the little one. "Yes, I'm the guy on that show. My name is Derek."

"No it isn't. My mommy calls you Hall Pass."

We all busted out laughing. Her poor mortified mother overheard and rushed over. "Katie! Oh dear, I'm terribly sorry. I don't know what she is talking about. Katie, let's go have Corky the Clown paint your face."

As she dragged Katie to the kiddy side of the party the little girl said, "He says his name is Derek. Mommy, what's a Hall Pass?"

Katie broke the ice. All of Steve and Scott's work friends came over to get their picture with Derek. He, of course, happily obliged. He warned me not to go very far and tortured me via remote.

The pulse waves rumbling through my body were too much. I got Derek's attention, and ran into the house. One thing needed to get off—my panties or me. I wasn't sure which would be first.

I ran upstairs to our bedroom consumed with need.

I tore off my clothes, including the torture panties. Where the heck was Derek? My body yearned for its spanking. Nothing else could extinguish the deviant craving between my legs.

When I lay on the bed, my head spun. I was a little drunk, and giggled to myself. Here I was flat on my back, naked and alone, while hosting an enormous party.

I looked down at my pert little wonders. My nipples were so hard they could've cut glass. I imagined myself handcuffed to the bed and Derek using those nipple clamps. I never thought I'd like anything like that, but with Derek, I wanted to experience everything.

I encircled and pinched the taut pebbles and sighed. God, where was Derek? I needed to come so bad, it was almost painful. My hands drifted down my waist and landed on my slushy slit. I closed my eyes and gave in as I pressed two fingers inside my expectant channel.

"Well, well, well… What do we have here? Did you start without me?"

I flipped my eyes open. "No, I was, um… Yes, okay yes. Derek, those damn panties were excruciating. Please?"

He ripped off his clothes. "Please, what?"

"Please, make me come. Please, spank me. Please, fuck me to the moon and back."

He cupped my face with his gorgeous hands. "Only if you insist."

"I fucking insist!"

He gave me that look and sat with his back resting against the headboard. He spread his legs and motioned for me to sit between them. I rested my back against his front. He brushed my hair to one side and grazed his fingers along my cheekbone and down my neck. I exhaled. Just the simplest touch nearly sent me flying.

One hand palmed my breast, the other rested on my welcoming pussy. He gripped me tight. "Don't move, baby. Let me make you come."

His exquisite fingers were flush against my swollen clit, rubbing me lightly. He skated over my slickness. I was delirious with need. My creamy wetness demanded more and bucked against his hand, in its frenzied pursuit of orgasm. He took his hand away and whispered, "Hold still, my greedy girl. Just relax."

I melded into him and spread myself wider.

He nuzzled my neck. "That's it. I want you to watch. Watch me make you come."

Finally, he pushed two fingers deep inside and I moaned in relief. I watched him play me like a well-tuned instrument. It was all about that bass as he conducted my body toward booming acclaim. He strummed me with full-toned notes, sweeping along my hot spot. A swell of crescendos beat within, flinging me to greater elevations, orchestrating a deluge of pleasure moans. He struck a vibrant chord within me, exalting my desire with measured movements.

His clever fingers continued treating me to a session of rhythmic perfection. "You feel ready. Let me see your cum. Spray my hand."

He brought his soaking fingers to my engorged bud, and his other hand parted my outer lips. He spanked my pussy with expert staccato taps and my arousal squirted forth like a waterfall. It was a glorious, tawdry sight.

"Look what a good girl you are. I fucking love it."

Derek vigorously rubbed my clit, taking me to my final shrieking, wailing, *squirtacular* destination.

My body heaved and wilted into him. I angled my face to his. "That was awesome. Thank you. I feel so much better now."

He calmed my hypersensitive flesh with his hand. "You're the one who's awesome."

I gave him a quick kiss, and moved to my hands and knees to reach for my dress.

Derek stopped me. "Where do you think you're going?"

"I'm getting dressed. We have a backyard full of people."

"I don't think so."

He grabbed me around the waist and hauled me over his knee. Oh man, my ass was about to be spanked. My body responded immediately with renewed dampness pooling between my legs. But, we were hosting a party for fuck's sake.

"Derek, we can't do this right now."

"Is that an argument? Do you want to add to your punishment?" He ran his fingers the length of my crack crease, awakening every nerve ending. Maybe no one would miss us. I opened my legs wider so he could access every part of me.

"Hmm…that's better. Look at this beautiful ass begging for discipline. You've been a very naughty girl, Nia Kelly." His hands fondled my bottom as he listed my offenses. "First, you didn't save all your pleasure for me. Then, you purposely went out of range of the remote. And if I'm not mistaken, you're a little drunk."

"You forgot I called you an old guy."

A surprise crack landed on each unsuspecting cheek.

I yelped.

"Just for that, young lady, I'm going to pretend it's your twenty-sixth birthday."

"What do you mean?"

"Twenty six spankings on your pretend birthday. That should do nicely for a fire-engine red behind." His hand teased my juicy center, creating a deep heat in my pulsating core. "Oh, and if you come before I get to twenty-six, just consider it your thirtieth birthday."

My breath caught in my throat. I was totally screwed. I would never hold out that long. But I thrived on a good challenge. He had me in some kind of sensual haze. I didn't care if he pretended it was my twenty-sixth, my thirtieth, or my hundredth birthday, with my face plastered on a jar of *Smucker's* jelly.

I peered over my shoulder and wiggled my wayward ass in his face. "Give it to me."

He growled, with a hint of a grin. "Such a bad girl."

My defenseless bottom lay in wait, while everything else prickled and pulsed. He placed a firm hand on the small of my back and then thwack, five sharp blows! His fingers delved between my legs to investigate my plump silkiness. That was only five and I was already veering toward the edge. His bulging erection dug into my stomach, increasing my arousal.

Five more slaps followed. That was Derek's pattern. He'd go back and forth between cheeks and the fifth landed on my crack. Each time his hand worked me to the fringe a little longer. His twentieth spank reduced me to a quaking heap of decadent rapture. His fingers pumped me full throttle. There was no escaping my determined, tenacious release. I gushed like a river while my groans of fulfillment resonated in the room.

Derek grunted. "You naughty girl, you're coming."

"Yes. Oh God ah…"

"Ten more spankings for you."

"Oh please, yes."

Ten quick, softer slaps ensued as his hand drained my pussy of every ounce of sprinkling revelry.

My burning ass couldn't move, nor could the rest of me. Still reeling, I exhaled. "I'm sorry."

He helped me up and tucked me next to him. "What on earth are you sorry for? Sweetie, you're amazing."

"You told me not to come until you got to twenty-six."

He chuckled a bit. "I was just messing with you. I knew you wouldn't be able to hold out."

"Well, that's a very risky little game, Mr. Pierce."

He brushed my hair off my face, his voice laced with seduction. "Do you like it when we play little games in the bedroom?"

"I do."

"Say that again."

"*I do.*"

"God, I can't wait to marry you."

Derek pressed his lips against my forehead before taking my mouth. We settled into sweet, gentle kisses that warmed to my depths. His tongue slid inside and met with mine. A low moan rumbled from the back of his throat as he climbed on top of me.

He broke our kiss and gazed into my eyes. "I have to be inside you. I've been going crazy all night craving you, wanting you."

I thrust my hands in his hair, drawing him to my lips, and opened up to him. My appetite for Derek was limitless, a boundless flaming hunger. His abundant immersion whisked us away to the hereafter. He vehemently shafted me to his root in an outpouring of galvanizing strokes. *Hell yes!* He fucked me to the moon and back.

For a moment, I felt like the worst hostess ever, abandoning my guests to satisfy our desires. But right before I came undone beneath Derek, I decided those party people could suck it!

Suddenly the music outside stopped. We jerked up and froze. The DJ's voice boomed over the microphone. "Steve and Scott will be making a toast after the slow dancing portion of the evening. So grab your honey and come to the dance floor."

Derek handed me my dress. "We better get back out there."

"Yeah, we should. We wouldn't want people to gossip about us. Apparently, there's enough of that already going on in the tabloids. Is there anything you need to tell me?"

All night long, I had the strangest vibe something was going on. Maybe the vibrating panties were supposed to distract me.

He pulled on his shorts. "Nothing for you to worry about."

What the hell did that mean? I clammed up, threw on my dress, and trekked to my dresser for a fresh, dry thong.

Derek came to me and placed his hands on my shoulders. "Nia, look at me. Do you trust me?"

I looked at him, all of him, the small crease between his brow that furrowed when he stressed, his soft kissable lips that said he loved me, his ice-blue eyes that held me in his heart, and his strong arms that protected me and kept me safe. "Yes, I trust you."

"Do you love me and know that I would never do anything to hurt you?"

"Yes."

He caressed my face. "Then nothing else matters. It's all white noise. Let's go."

"Okay, but give a girl a chance to get her panties on."

The mood shifted back to playful. He led me back to the bed. "I'm afraid I can't let you do that. Once I spank an ass, it remains commando."

I giggled. "Have you spanked many asses in your day, you know, back when dinosaurs roamed the earth?"

He pressed his body to mine. "You're a bad girl, Nia Kelly. I'm tempted to keep you in here all night and fuck the naughty out of you."

"You could try."

"I intend to. And to answer your question, I have only spanked one ass, yours. I plan to take excellent care of it. Lay on the bed, sweetie, on your stomach."

He had a plan, for my ass? I happily complied!

Derek sat down on the bed next me and lifted my dress up, exposing my freshly spanked bottom. He grabbed the lavender lotion on my nightstand and rubbed it gently all over my behind. It was so tranquil and serene. Derek gave me light kisses on the small of my back and pulled my dress down. "There, all better."

"Julia's probably ready to send out a search party for us. I guess we'd better head out."

Derek helped me up and snaked his arms around my waist. "Can you do me a favor? Can you eat something for me?"

He was right. I pounded several white wines in the heat, on an empty stomach. I smiled. "Whatever you say, Mr. Pierce."

He grinned wickedly. "Well, if that's the case, the next time I catch you starting without me, I will watch you finish without me."

*Oh, Christ on a cracker!* He wanted to watch me masturbate. I looked away a little flushed. "I thought you said only you could make me come."

With one long finger, he tipped my chin so our eyes met. "Well, you gave me a little preview tonight and I'd like to see the whole show. Sweetie, you still have no idea how incredibly sexy you are. Watching you make yourself come would be fucking hot."

How did he do that? How did he put me at ease and make me aroused, all in a few words?

"Maybe I'll fuck the naughty out of myself."

"I'm starting think that's not even possible. Come. Let's head back to the party."

* * * *

We popped in the kitchen for a bite to eat. The sun had set when we returned to the party. Steve and Scott's friends with little kids left, along with Corky the Clown. Surprisingly, Tiffany the stilt walker changed clothes and joined the party. She stood next to the deflated bouncy house, chatting up Walter and sucking on a snow cone. *Could she be more obvious? Why not duck behind the cotton candy machine and blow him?*

The song, "The Rhythm of Love" played while most of the guests danced. The chorus girls, Nancy and Sharon came without their husbands, so they paired off with Steve and Scott. Jeff and Sue swayed close by, and Brooke and Tom were out there too. Lacey's smile beamed from across the yard as she danced with a very tall man. Good for her. Julia and Phillip hung out with Shannon at the bar. Shannon leered at Tiffany and Walter with slumped shoulders. I encouraged Derek to ask her to dance. Once they were out on the dance floor, Julia grilled me.

"Nia Kelly, where have you and Derek been?"

"Phillip, cover your ears if you don't want to hear this. I'm about to tell your wife the filthy truth."

"I knew it."

"Knew what?" Phillip asked.

"Remember the naughty bridal shower I threw Nia?" Julia said. "She was wearing my gift, the vibrating panties."

"Oh, remind me, I have to run a panty errand tomorrow."

We chuckled and joined everyone on the dance floor.

The DJ took to the microphone. "For the last song of the night we have a special request."

He played, "That's What Friends Are For."

It was completely cheesy and sweet. We stood in a

circle, held hands and sang along, except for Walter and Tiffany. Either she was blowing him behind the cotton candy machine, or they'd left.

After the song was over the DJ handed the microphone to Scott who in turn gave it to Steve, since he enjoyed the spotlight. "Before we go, Scott and I wanted to thank you all for coming, and thank our gracious hosts, Nia and Derek. You know the night they met, we saw Nia at Julia's house. I remember her saying she made such an ass of herself, she could never watch another episode of *First Bite,* ever again. But we knew they'd end up together."

Scott hijacked the mic. "Now, if Tom proposes to Brooke, we would feel like our work here is done."

Everyone whooped it up. Brooke died from embarrassment, but Tom didn't flinch. It made me curious.

When they finished their speech, they came over to say goodnight. Tears welled in my eyes.

Scott said, "Okay, Lady Boo Hoo, no tears. If you start crying, then I'll start crying."

I pulled myself together. "I'm really going to miss you guys."

Steve chimed in, "I know. We're pretty great."

They gave me a big hug and Steve said to Derek, "Take care of our girl for us."

"You have my word. I promise to take good care of her, and never let her go."

Unfortunately, I had to let Steve and Scott go. We

all embraced one final time and I told them I loved them. I couldn't bear to say goodbye, so instead I said, "See you soon."

# Chapter Seven

I woke to a pounding headache, and an "alarm cock" digging in my back.

"Good morning, sweet girl, are you awake?"

I opened one eye and squinted at the clock. "No. It's only six o'clock. It's too early."

He kissed the back of my neck, moving to my shoulder. I was way too hungover for morning sex.

"Honey, my head hurts. I drank too much wine."

After our goodbye to Steve and Scott, we walked over to Julia's to pick up Molly. We weren't planning to stay, but one bottle of wine led to the next. I should've stuck to the plan.

Derek had little sympathy for me. "I believe I mentioned someone was too little to consume so much alcohol and you would be hungover in the morning."

"Apparently, I was too drunk to hear you. I'm sorry. I promise I will never over serve myself again. I feel like shit. Are you mad?"

"No, but you might be when I teach you to swim this morning if your headache doesn't go away."

*Oh, fuck me!* This sucked. I pulled the pillow over my head. "Can't we do that tomorrow?"

He removed the pillow. "I'll make you a deal. I'll take Molly for a run before it gets too hot, and you stay in bed. But when I get back, put on the swimsuit I sent you, and come down to the pool. Sound good?"

"Sure, we could do that. Or we could do *anything* else."

He smiled and kissed my forehead. "Feel better, sweetie. I'll be right back."

* * * *

I slept until ten o'clock. Thank God my hangover subsided. I put on the ugly ass one-piece light-grey bathing suit and all the equally odd swimming accessories—like the white bathing cap and matching water wings. I looked beyond ridiculous. Derek came in the bedroom with Molly tagging along. He took one glance at me and bit his lip to keep from laughing.

"Okay, that's it. There is no way I'm wearing this. I look like a deranged *Q-tip*." Molly let out a loud guttural yawn and we cracked up. It was as if she couldn't bear my silly ensemble.

"All right, you win. Take it off."

"Gladly." I peeled off the swim cap and shook out my hair. Perhaps I could delay the inevitable by performing a sexy striptease. I slid each water wing to my wrists as if they were long white gloves. I reached my hands behind my neck to untie the suit and then that happened. The stupid water wings rubbed together and made a noise. It sounded like a fart!

"Oh, my God, this is so not sexy!"

Derek was laughing so hard he could barely speak. "Did you just fart?"

"No! It's the stupid water wings, see." I rubbed them together. They made the noise again, and Molly ran out of the room. We busted a gut.

Derek came to me and wrapped me up in his arms. "God, I love you. All right, my little *Q-tip*. Put your bikini on and meet me at the pool in ten minutes."

The mood shifted when I looked up at him and nodded.

I swallowed hard. "You promise you won't let go."

He held me a little tighter. "I will never let go."

* * * *

"Let's get you used to the water first," Derek said in his soothing voice. He sat on the first step of the swimming pool. I straddled him with my arms clinging around his neck. He trickled the water over my shoulders and back, while I nuzzled my cheek against his chest. It was already a hundred degrees. The water refreshed my warm skin.

"I'm going to slide down to the next step, okay, sweetie?"

"Okay, I'm ready."

We submerged deeper and a splash of water caused me to gasp.

Derek tightened his grip on me. "Are you still all right?"

I peered up at him and the expression in his eyes threw me.

"Honey, are you all right?"

He smoothed some water over my hair. "Yeah, I was just thinking about you. You know, when your mom died... I love you so much, it tears me up inside to think about you being twelve years old, losing your mom and feeling all alone in the world."

In that moment, his sweet vulnerability and love for me gave me strength. "But I'm not alone anymore. I have you. Your love makes me brave, like I can do anything, like we can do anything. And you know what, if Mom was here right now, she would tell me to quit being such a baby and dunk my head in the water." I rose and opened my arms to him. "So, teacher, I'm all yours."

Derek smiled and took my hands. "Okay, first up, I want you to hang onto the side of the pool and blow bubbles."

"If I blow anything else, do I get extra credit?"

"You're already being naughty and the lesson hasn't even started yet. I love it."

"I was hoping you'd make me stay after class for the skinny-dipping portion of the program."

He patted my ass. "I'm sure that can be arranged."

"Ouch. It still smarts from last night."

"Seriously? Pull your bottoms down, let me take a look."

I peeled off my bottoms and he examined my

cheeks. "Hmm…it looks okay, perfect as usual."

I pulled them back up. "Psyche."

"I should've known. Come on, no more stalling."

Derek took me to side of the pool and instructed me to hang onto the edge. Sure enough, I was blowing bubbles. Then I clung to the side and kicked my legs. I didn't have the most buoyant body. Perhaps I should've brought those water wings to the pool. Instead, Derek kept one hand on my stomach and one hand on my back. Once I straightened out my legs and quit flapping them about, I did much better. He taught me what to do with my arms, by demonstrating a basic stroke. I was ready to put it all together when Molly jumped in the water and swam to Derek with the ease and grace of a dolphin.

I quipped, "Show off."

"Molly, you're stealing Mommy's thunder."

After a quick cool off, our little black puppy climbed out of the pool and trotted off to her hoarder tree.

Now it was my turn to display my skills.

Derek was such a good coach. "You can do this, sweetie, push off and swim to me."

I pushed off the side of the pool. Holy crap! I was swimming. I probably looked like a dork, but I felt like an Olympian. Derek cheered me on and when I got to him, he scooped me up in his arms.

"You did it. I'm so proud of you."

"Let's do it again."

We spent the next hour swimming, splashing, and frolicking in the water. I loved it. It was such good cardio.

I got out for a moment to check on Molly and when I got back in the water, Derek had that look. If he wanted to have pool sex, I was all for it. I'd never done it before. I untied my bikini top and chucked it. Then his swim trunks flew out of the pool. He pulled me close and I coiled my legs around his waist. I loved the weightless feeling of the water. The sensation was out of this world. Once Derek rid me of my bikini bottoms, he slid inside. We floated away on our desire for one another.

The water used to represent extreme anguish and sorrow. It held me captive in fear. But now I was in Derek's arms and no longer afraid. As we climaxed together, our connection unfurled, reaching a deeper, more intimate level. Our love bloomed and flourished. It was stronger than ever.

* * * *

"Derek didn't want me to say anything, but there's a story about him and Lena Rozwell that's gone viral. I'm sure it isn't true, but I thought you should know. You know the code, hos before bros. Let me know if you need to talk or anything."

My jaw hit the floor after I read Shannon's text. Lena Rozwell was the model who threw herself at

Derek in Paris two months ago. What the hell was going on?

Derek was outside bathing Molly with the hose, so I dashed to his office and clicked on his computer. I didn't even have to search for it. It was on the computer's home page.

"Lena Rozwell is shocked by Derek Pierce's recent engagement. She claims not long ago she was naked in his bed in Paris."

There was also a video of her talking to the paparazzi outside a trendy hot spot, making the same statement. All the entertainment shows picked up the story. Oh, my God, it made me sick.

Derek popped his head in the office. "I gave Molly a bath. She's lying on a towel outside on the grass."

I sat there, dumbfounded. Did Derek know this story was out there and not tell me?

He came to me. "Sweetie, what's wrong?"

Remaining calm, I responded, referring to the computer screen. "It's this. Lena Rozwell says she was naked in your bed in Paris. The story is everywhere."

He hung his head. "How did you find out about this?"

"How could you know about this and not tell me?"

The sudden realization everyone knew hit me like a punch in the gut. Maybe it was the real reason he wrote my friends thank-you notes, so he could tell them not to say anything.

"Derek, did you ask my friends not to tell me about

this?"

He exhaled. "Yes."

I fled to the door and he blocked me. "Nia, wait. You need to stop for a second and listen. When Lena put this story out, it was a tiny blip on the radar. No one paid her any attention, so she kept saying it until the media machine ate it up and spat it out. I was trying to protect you. I signed up for this kind of bullshit, you didn't. I thought it if you didn't find out about it then you wouldn't get hurt."

"Except, now I am hurt. I'm hurt that you lied to me. I knew something was going on. I even asked you last night if there was anything you had to tell me and you said nothing."

"I said there was nothing you needed to worry about."

I swallowed hard and braced myself. "Is it true? Was she naked in your bed in Paris?"

Derek stared at the floor. "I'm afraid so."

Tears welled up. "How could you?"

"Nia, nothing happened. I told you that. She threw herself at me and I rejected her." He reached for my hand and I recoiled.

"Yes, I guess you did tell me. You just left out a pesky little detail about her being naked in your bed. Who were you really protecting, me or you?"

I bolted toward the stairs. When I got to the landing, he grabbed my arms. An image of Nick and I fighting flashed in my mind and I screamed.

He released me. "I'm sorry. Just let me explain. We can't let this stupid shit drive you away from me."

"Stupid shit? You think this is stupid shit. You need to let me explain something. If you'd told me the whole truth about Paris and Lena planting a story, this wouldn't even be an issue. Not telling me is not protecting me. It is betraying me. Do you get that?"

I was halfway down the stairs, and Derek shouted, "Nia, don't go. I get it, I fucked-up, but don't run away."

When he accused me of running away, it struck a nerve. From the bottom of the steps, I yelled, "I am not running away. You are pushing me away. Last night at the party, everyone knew about this but me. Now I feel like an idiot. You did that. I am humiliated."

* * * *

"I can't believe Shannon sent you that text," Julia said as she handed me a glass of water.

"I'm sure she had my best interest at heart. You know, hos before bros."

"You do realize you're automatically giving Shannon the benefit of the doubt, and not Derek?"

Julia liked to play devil's advocate. Normally I appreciated her advice, but I was so angry, I couldn't absorb it.

"I don't know how you can defend him. He purposely asked you to keep this from me. Don't you think that was a total dick move?"

"No, I don't, and here's why. I know without a doubt Derek loves you. He would never do anything to hurt you intentionally. I have complete faith in him. Why don't you?"

"What? Are you on his side?"

"I'm not on anyone's side. But I think you need to put yourself in his shoes. He must be torn up over this. The more he tried to protect you, the more it blew up in his face."

"I can't believe you're saying this. He betrayed me and I'm supposed to let it go?"

Julia crossed her arms and spoke in her "I'm always right" voice. "Betrayed is a strong word. You're completely overreacting."

"What the hell? I came to you for help."

"I know, and I'm trying to help you. The hard truth is, you have a famous person problem. No offense, but it's not an actual problem."

I stormed to the front door. "I'm so done with this conversation."

Julia followed me. "Go ahead, leave, don't listen to me. But I'm right and you know it."

"I told you I'm done. If you want to keep running your mouth, talk to my balls, because I'm out!"

"I would love to, but first you need to grow a pair. You had better buck up. Life in the public eye isn't going to get any easier. If you don't believe in him and what you two have, your relationship will crumble."

I said nothing as I slammed the door, fuming the entire way home. Without a word to Derek, I marched up the stairs to take a shower. Julia's words echoed through my mind. Damn it, could she be right, again? I immediately thought the worst of Derek. If I allowed every tabloid article to upset me, we would fall apart. Maybe I did need to "grow a pair." Oh, God, I told Julia to talk to my balls. Sometimes my mouth surprised even me.

The bathroom door creaked open as I rinsed out the conditioner. Derek stepped behind me in the shower. Very gingerly, his arms caressed my waist. I closed my eyes, sensing his pain. His silence and the way he held me spoke volumes. This man would move heaven and earth to protect me. He already had.

I turned, and met his gaze. "I'm sorry."

Relief washed over him. "I am too. It crushed me to see you hurt. I can't take it. You ran away."

"It won't happen again."

"You're right, it won't."

With nostrils flaring, he pressed me against the wall. "Running away is no longer an option. You'll stay with me and we'll fight it out, figure it out, or fuck it out, understand?"

He grabbed my wrists and pinned them above my head. His mouth seized mine, stealing the breath from my lungs. His kisses dominated my being, and intensified the fevered sensation already coursing through my veins.

He released me and captured my chin. "Do you understand?" Two fingers plunged inside.

I gasped. "Yes, yes… I…understand."

The combination of his demanding mouth and his firm hand taking what was his forced me to the cusp. I thrashed against the wall in burgeoning euphoria.

Derek slowed his assault. "Look at me. Are you close?"

"Yes."

He rested his forehead on mine. "Good. I'm going to keep you there. Eyes on me."

His hooded glare burrowed into me. The water flowed over us in rivulets, plastering his hair to his face. His lips hovered over mine. Tiny droplets of moisture dribbled into my mouth while I panted, and whimpered.

He granted me just enough of his delicious finger rubs to keep me teetering on the brink. It transported me to an indescribable state that gripped me with electrifying intensity. He held me there, evoking a newfound ecstasy. My cunt flesh trembled in impassioned pleas.

He merged our lips together in a fervent, soul-melding kiss. "You are mine. I am yours. I'm never letting go."

His cock tore into me and I toppled over the edge, screaming his name. He slammed into me repeatedly, as a fresh set of tremors hummed inside.

The way he fucked me was the way he loved me. It was all consuming, unapologetic, and relentless. He was right. Everything else was just white noise. This was what mattered. I wasn't running. We were going to fight it out, figure it out, or fuck it out. I preferred the latter.

* * * *

Blissful snuggling in bed followed our primal make-up sex. My body felt like a bowl of limp noodles, but in a splendid, freshly fucked way.

Derek's squeezed me so tight. I teased, "Wow, you really aren't going to let me go, are you?"

"Never. By the way, I know you went to Julia's house. When you left, she called me and said you were so mad you told her to talk to your balls."

"It wasn't one of my finer moments, but she took your side, and it felt like she kicked me in the nuts."

"She took my side?"

"Yes, she always does. She said I need to believe in you, and you would never intentionally hurt me… blah…blah…blah."

"I really should start buying Julia more presents."

I elbowed him and we chuckled. Of course, I owed Julia an apology, but first I had one more question for Derek.

"Derek, can I ask you something?"

He took my hands in his. "Of course, anything."

"How did Lena end up naked in your bed?"

"Remember the dress I bought you in Paris? The

one you wore the night Nick—

"Anyway, the night before the photo shoot, I wasn't in my room because I was shopping for your dress. Lena convinced the front desk we were a couple. She told them she had a surprise for me, so they let her in my room. When I got there, she was naked, in my bed, and I was furious. I told her to get the hell out. Then I went to the front desk and, it wasn't pretty."

"Why would she purposely plant it in the media?"

"I talked to my publicist, Aaron, and he said she hasn't worked since Paris. Word got out how difficult she was on set and no one will touch her. So if she can spin something, anything, it might keep her relevant."

"That's just so sick."

"I know. It's amazing what people will do if they're desperate for attention, which brings me to Oliver."

Oh great! Oliver Rock, Derek's cast mate on *First Bite*. I managed to avoid him at all *First Bite* functions after he kissed me the same weekend Lena pulled her stunt on Derek. Those two were made for each other.

"What about Oliver?"

"Aaron was concerned Oliver would latch on to Sophia's story, by letting the world know he kissed you. Luckily, he isn't. Being rejected and slapped by Derek Pierce's girlfriend isn't something he wants anyone to know. It means, there is at least one woman in the world that can resist him."

"I hope I never see him again. He gives me the

creeps."

"I'll have to invite him to our engagement party. I'm inviting the whole cast, but I don't think he'll come."

"If he does, I have no problem kicking his ass, again. I could totally take him."

"I don't doubt my little slugger for a moment."

Derek paused. He released my hands and smoothed the hair off my face. "I need you to do something for me. Before you say no, just hear me out."

"Derek, you're scaring me. What is it?"

"Aaron thought it would be a good idea if you joined me on the red carpet next week, when my movie premieres in LA."

Another red carpet was the last thing I wanted to do. The first time was a blast, but in general, I wasn't a fan of LA. I preferred staying in Vegas and out of the spotlight.

I mumbled, "Do I have to?"

"I'm afraid if you're not with me it will look like there's more to Lena's claims. At first, we thought it was best to stay silent. Then the story would die out, but it isn't happening. So, we'll go, show a united front and that will be our statement. Please, my angel, do this for me? I know it makes you uncomfortable, but think of it as a fancy date night. And the next day, I will take you shopping for a dress for our engagement party, and anything else your heart desires. I plan on spoiling you rotten."

"Well, as long as you have a plan then, yes."

He drew me onto his lap. "Thank you, I promise you'll have the time of your life."

# Chapter Eight

"Get out of the shot, move." An angry mob of media vultures taunted me.

We were on the red carpet for Derek's premiere of *Fourth of July*. Aaron and Derek begged me to walk the carpet, and now the press harassed me. They demanded pictures of Derek, alone. Why did I bother squeezing myself into this uncomfortable borrowed gown? It was absolute chaos. The stale air swirled around us, while sweat trickled down my back. The press's verbal assaults were relentless. I'd rather lick a dirty *Tic Tac* than be here another moment. Derek kept a firm grip on my hand until Aaron tapped his shoulder and nodded. It was like some secret, red carpet, coaching code. I was being taken out of the game.

Derek whispered to me, "I need to give the press what they want. Can you back away and stand with Aaron?"

I was relieved and happy to oblige, but as he released my hand, something shifted. It was slight, like a microscopic flicker, a tiny cosmic flutter. A tear escaped my left eye and Aaron caught me discretely wiping it away.

He said in a stern voice, for my ears only. "Nia, you can't show any emotion. I know this is overwhelming, but I need you to slap a smile on your face and gaze lovingly at your fiancé. He's doing his job."

I smiled through gritted teeth. "I didn't want to come at all. This was your idea."

"Exactly, you need to be here and be invisible. It's not about you. It's about Derek and his career. You're not just marrying him, you're marrying all of this. Welcome to the fucked-up media machine known as Hollywood. Don't let him down."

The bitter truth of Aaron's statement sunk in. This was a huge slice of Derek's world. By comparison, our life in Vegas was a whimsical fairy tale. Vegas Derek was attentive, sweet, and relaxed. LA Derek was stressed, distracted, and short-tempered.

Julia's words flooded back to me. I needed to "grow a pair." Before I left for LA, we both apologized for our spat. Turns out, Julia and Phillip were struggling with infertility issues. They'd been trying to get pregnant much longer than anyone knew. No wonder she had zero patience for my famous person problem. We had a good laugh about me telling her to talk to my balls. I closed my eyes for an instant and focused on Julia's laugh. She was always there for me, even now on this out of control red carpet. I slapped a smile on my face and gazed lovingly at my fiancé. Perhaps I was ready for my balls now.

* * * *

Derek's face filled with tension as the lights dimmed and the credits rolled. He hadn't uttered a word to me since he told me to back away and stand with Aaron.

I didn't understand. The *First Bite* premiere rocked. Everyone was easygoing and ready to party. Was I at a funeral or a movie? Why didn't I stay in Vegas? This wasn't a fancy date night. This was turning into a disaster.

The dawn broke about halfway through the film. *Fourth of July* sucked ass. The jokes fell flat and the plot jumped around with little cohesion. Even the people in the movie didn't watch it. Everyone was on their phone, some left. Derek garnered top billing as one of the stars, but had little screen time.

He said to Aaron, "They've cut my storyline to shreds. This is ridiculous. It makes no sense."

He jerked out of his seat. "Come on, were leaving."

* * * *

The ride home in the limo was nearly as bad as the movie. Derek conference called his team. Tempers ran high as they sorted out this heaping pile of crap. From what I could gather, Derek never wanted to do *Fourth of July*. His team talked him into it. They said the good buzz of this movie would help with the distribution and box office of his independent film, *Traitors in Our*

*Midst*. Now, Derek had his name attached to one of the biggest flops of the summer. I'd never seen him so angry and cold. I didn't feel my connection to him. It was just as Aaron said. I was invisible.

* * * *

Derek's frustration was palpable when we got to the bedroom. I sat on the edge of the bed afraid to ask him to unzip my dress. I was afraid to say a word. He ripped off his tie and hurled it across the room. His hands rubbed the back of his neck.

He exhaled. "I'm sorry."

"I'm sorry you're so upset. Is it because they cut you out of the movie? Maybe that's a good thing, since it—"

"Sucks?" He raised his voice. "Is that the word you're looking for?"

Damn it! Why did I say that?

"Nia, you just don't get it. What a colossal fucked-up mess."

He marched to the bathroom and slammed the door. This was total bullshit. Maybe I didn't understand, but I didn't deserve this. It was time for Derek to grow a pair.

I pounded on the door and yelled, "You know what else is fucked-up? You! You're acting like a big baby. And another thing, I'm never, ever walking the red carpet again. Some fancy date night. The press screamed at me and you didn't speak to me all night. And for the love of God, will you stop being so self-involved and get me out of this mother-fucking dress."

The door flew open and Derek's icy-blue eyes fumed. He spun me around and unzipped me with lightening speed. Adrenaline fired through me, as I stepped out of my dress and steadied myself.

"When I was in the limo tonight I almost asked you to take me to the airport so I could go home. But you told me I couldn't run away anymore. What's it going to be, Derek? Are we going to fight it out, figure it out, or fuck it out? I'm staying, I'm not going anywhere."

"Go ahead, stay. I'm sleeping in the guest room."

I said nothing as he walked out and shut the door. What the hell happened? I was willing to stick it out and fight for us, but Derek wasn't. He ran away.

* * * *

I woke to a quiet house and combed his entire mansion searching for him. I was alone, no Derek, or his housekeeper, David. Derek was right about one thing. This was one colossal fucked-up mess.

My heart leaped when a voice called my name. I raced downstairs to find Keith, Derek's assistant. What a welcome sight. Keith and Tim, his partner, were back from their vacation.

The second I hugged him, tears burned my eyes.

"I'm so glad to see you. Derek and I had this

horrible fight and—"

"Oh trust me, I already know all about it."

"You do?"

He took my hand and led me to the kitchen. "Yeah, and I let him have it. Every once in a while Derek needs a good kick in the ass."

"I've never seen him so angry."

I sat on the kitchen island, and Keith went to the refrigerator. Knowing Derek, he probably told Keith to make me breakfast.

He poured me orange juice. "It's this business. It gets to everybody, even someone successful like Derek. Everyone thinks they're one bad movie away from the unemployment line."

"Then the cast of *Fourth of July* needs to line up."

"Was it really that bad?"

"Don't tell Derek, but it was one of the worst movies I wished I'd never seen."

"I believe you. The reviews are in and it's not good. Derek's with his team strategizing. He'll be in meetings all day."

"Let me guess, you're my stunt date."

"You got it, girl."


* * * *


Decked out from head to toe, Keith and I zoomed to Beverly Hills in Derek's Porsche.

He was a hoot to shop with and a pleasant

distraction after the blow up with Derek. Between Keith, the new white dress for the engagement party, and three pairs of divine shoes, the day brightened.

Derek's Porsche slid perfectly into an ideal parking spot outside the restaurant. We scored a superb table on the patio for lunch. I could people watch, and Keith could keep and eye on Derek's car.

Admiring my engagement ring, Keith said, "That's one fabulous ring. I know Derek acted a fool, but he loves you. When he called me this morning I could tell he knew he blew it. He's really sorry."

"Sometimes I'm at a loss. I want to have faith in us, but it's tough. I know his career is everything to him, he's worked so hard, but to me it's like a cruel mistress that keeps hurting us."

"Show business isn't just a cruel mistress. It's also a dirty whore who won't quit stalking your ass."

I giggled and dove into my overpriced salad. Keith brought his water glass to his lips. Without taking a drink, he slapped it back on the table.

The expression on his face frightened me. "Keith, are you okay?"

"Oh, hell no." He leaned in. "You know how Derek doesn't want any women working for him?"

"Yeah, why is that? He won't tell me."

"Don't look, but the reason he doesn't is headed this way. Good Lord, please don't let her see me."

"Keith? Keith Johnson? Is that you?" a smoky voice said behind me.

Keith responded tentatively, "Oh, hey, Jackie. It's been forever. I almost didn't recognize you... Uh... Nia, this is Jackie Berman. She used to...um...work for Derek."

I'd never seen Keith so frazzled. Granted, Jackie possessed an intimidating stance and looked like she'd been in a few bar fights, but why was Keith so awkward? Obviously, this situation was one more thing Derek didn't tell me. Was she an ex? We couldn't be more different. She was tall and masculine with dyed jet-black hair and heavy makeup.

I extended my hand. "Nice to meet you, Jackie."

"Yeah, wait, what's your name again?"

"It's Nia, Nia Kelly."

Her suspicious eyes spied my engagement ring. "Are you Derek's fiancée? I heard he got engaged, but I didn't believe it. Let me guess, you have no idea who I am, do you?"

Keith interrupted, "Sure, she knows you worked for Derek. Anyway, we were going to get the check and head out. It was nice to see you."

She leaned on the railing. "It was nice to meet you, Nia. Good luck with Derek, you're going to need it."

What was wrong with this woman? What a psycho. Before I could say anything, she recognized Derek's car. "I see Derek still has his Porsche. It's a great car. I love mine. Is it still the only car he let's anyone drive?"

For some stupid reason I opened up my giant mouth and lied my ass off. "No, it isn't. I drive all of

Derek's cars. In fact, after I drive us home in the Porsche, I'm busting out the Lamborghini, just because I can."

Keith shook his head and his eyes grew twice their size.

Jackie skimmed her fingers over the Porsche's tinted windows while an odd smile split her face.

"Drive safe," she replied and slithered away.

Keith rubbed his face. "Oh shit, oh shit, oh shit. Baby doll, we got to bounce." He sprang to his feet and threw some money on the table.

He jingled Derek's keys as we rushed out of the restaurant. "Did you really want to drive?"

"No, I guess I shouldn't have said that."

Before we peeled out of the parking spot, I grasped Keith's hand and begged, "Keith, what's going on? You have to tell me. What just happened?"

Keith stared at the steering wheel. "Jackie did work for Derek, and it didn't end well. I'm sorry, that's all I can say. You need to ask him."

I grabbed my cell phone. "Oh, I intend to."

He exhaled, muttering under his breath, "That bitch is some kind of serious crazy."

While he negotiated the traffic, my emotions ricocheted all over the place. Why didn't he tell me about Jackie? What was he hiding?

We idled at a red light when a text message from Derek popped up. It said, "I should be home in an hour. We need to talk. Love, Derek."

Did we ever, Captain Obvious. Before I wrote back, I lifted my head to tell Keith about the text. We pulled into the intersection, and it happened so fast. It was just like mom. A car ran a red light and sped toward us.

I screamed, "Keith!"

It smacked us hard on the driver's side and took off. The screeching and crunching of metal pierced my ears. The driver's side air bag deployed reverberating like a gunshot. I screamed for Keith, but he was still and silent. Oh, my God! There was so much blood!

I quickly called 911 and passersby came to our aid. I was hysterical.

A large man frantically opened my door. "Miss, are you okay?"

The siren whirled in the distance. I could barely get out any words. "Keith. He's not moving. Please help him."

Blood dripped in my right eye. Everything turned cloudy. I looked into the strange man's face, but couldn't focus.

He pressed a cloth to my head. "The ambulance is here. You'll be all right. I saw the whole thing. Jesus, that Porsche came out of nowhere."

# Chapter Nine

"I told you I'm fine. I need to find my friend." This was bullshit. Keith was in surgery and they wouldn't release me. I only suffered a minor head injury.

Derek flew through the emergency room doors.

I held my arms out to him. "Derek." He raced to my side and cradled me in his arms.

"Oh, sweetie. Thank God, you're okay."

A cry tore from my throat, "Keith's not okay. They took him to surgery. There was so much blood. It was just like my mom."

Images from both crashes flashed through my brain, the impact, the screams, and the blood. There was so much blood. I broke down in wailing sobs.

Derek blanketed me in his love and strength. "Shh…baby, it's okay. I'm right here… I've got you. You're okay and Keith is going to be okay too. I promise."

* * * *

As soon as I signed my release papers, we hurried to the surgical wing of the hospital. Tim paced in the small waiting area. Relief swept over his face when he saw us. His skin was ashen and his eyes were glassy.

My heart ached for him. His partner was in surgery fighting for his life.

It didn't make sense, but I couldn't shake the feeling that somehow this was my fault.

He embraced us. "I'm so glad to see you. I just talked to the surgeon and they were able to stop the internal bleeding. He lost a lot of blood, has a concussion, and his left hand is a mess, but he's going to be okay."

We erupted in joyful tears. I squeezed Tim tight. "When can we see him?"

"He's in recovery. As soon as a bed is available they're going to wheel him to a room."

"They'll take him to private room and they'll do it immediately." Derek said, "I'll be right back."

Derek worked his authoritative charm at the nurse's station.

Tim asked, "Nia, what happened? Are you all right?"

"Yeah, I'm fine, just a little foggy. We were at a red light and it turned green, and then *bam*. I didn't see it coming until it was too late."

Within moments, Keith settled into a lovely private room. Well, it was as lovely as a hospital room could be. The three of us sat and stared, willing him to open his eyes and crack us up like always.

Heavy footsteps made their way into Keith's room. Two officers, one with a protruding belly and sun-baked skin, the other was thin, bald, and smelled of cigarettes. They introduced themselves, but my pain meds kicked in so I thought of them as officer Belly and officer Baldy. Belly said there were several eyewitnesses, but everyone gave them a different color, make, and model of the car that hit us. Baldy explained that happened a lot and asked me what I remembered.

My brain remained jumbled. I told them a passerby helped me, and he said he saw the whole thing. He said something else. Damn it, why couldn't I remember? Belly and Baldy gave me their cards and I told them I'd call them if had more information.

After they left we hovered over Keith. His eyes fluttered searching to focus. Tim touched his forehead. "Keith, I'm here. Nia and Derek are too. You were in a car accident, but you're okay. Can you talk?"

"Am I still black and beautiful?"

Yes, Keith was going to be just fine.

* * * *

When we got home, Derek took exceptional care of me. He must've told me he loved me a hundred times and how sorry he was for last night. The shock of the accident put things in perspective. Life was fleeting. It could change on a dime. My own world shook and crashed many times. I bore the tattered scars inside and out to prove it. It nearly happened again today. Poor Keith was in a hospital bed. It could've been me. What if I'd been behind the wheel? It could've been me.

Instead, I was in Derek's luxurious king-size bed watching TV, longing to be in our bed in Vegas. I missed Molly, our puppy, and all my girls. As much as I didn't want a rehash of last night, there were things left unsaid. And what was the deal with nut bag, Jackie? It was essential I left no stone unturned. Even if my mind wasn't as clear as it should be.

Derek came into the room with my shopping bags.

"How in the world did you get those?"

"They towed the Porsche to Herb's Auto Shop and they called. The car's totaled, so I sent Bernie to pick up the contents. At least it wasn't a total loss."

"I'm sorry about your Porsche."

He sat next to me on the bed and drew my hand to his lips. "It's only a car. You, my sweet girl, are what matters the most. I'm going to spend the rest of my life making up for last night, if you'll let me."

"Derek, we need to talk."

"No, my baby needs to rest."

"Please."

Derek relented and switched off the TV, granting me his complete attention.

I exhaled. "I know you're sorry about last night, but I meant what I said. I'm not going to walk the red carpet again. In fact, I don't think I should come to LA anymore."

"Sweetie, please don't say that. I know things went off the rails last night, but it will never happen again. I promise."

"Don't make promises you can't keep. Something happens to you when you're here. Something happens to me too. I hate LA."

Derek ran his fingers through his hair in frustration. "But I have to be here. I can't believe you're doing this again. You're pushing me away."

An expression of defeat and hurt enslaved his face. It tore at my heart.

"I'm not pushing you away. I'm trying to save us. I would rather be in Vegas missing you, than be here and fight with you. It's going to destroy us."

The grim reality of our situation hunkered down between us. The room swarmed with a detectable tension.

Eventually Derek touched his lips to my forehead. "I love you. I'll do whatever it takes."

I swallowed hard and pressed on. "Then I need you to do something for me. I need you to tell me about Jackie Berman."

Just the mention of her named jolted Derek like he'd been hit by lightning. He jumped to his feet tramping about like a caged animal.

"I know she worked for you, and I met her today. I have to know what happened. She knows we're engaged and she kind of scares me."

"Did she hurt you?"

"No, but she said 'Good luck with Derek, you're going to need it.' What does that mean?"

Once he calmed down, he told me the entire awful

truth. Jackie was his housekeeper before David. The tabloids raked him over the coals after his breakup with Gisela. He was isolated from his cast and kept to himself. *First Bite* was shooting an episode that his character wasn't in, so he was home a lot and at loose ends. Jackie was sweet at first, making him special dinners, staying late and talking. Then one thing led to another and they slept together.

"You made love to her?"

"No, it was just sex. I'm sorry. I didn't tell you because I was ashamed. It was only once and I knew it was a mistake. Afterward I tried to reestablish our boundaries of boss and employee. But she said she was in love with me and that I took advantage of her. Then it all hit the fan. She became obsessed with my every move. Harassing phone calls, she'd show up on the lot. It was insane. I had no choice. I had to fire her."

"What did she do?"

"What do you think she did? She went ballistic. She threatened me with a lawsuit and said she was going to the press. Truth is she had a point. All anyone would see or hear was that I slept with her and fired her. The tabloids already blasted me because of Gisela. This could've buried me. So I threw money at the problem and she went away."

"How much money?"

He hesitated and finally muttered, "Two hundred thousand dollars."

*Fuck!* Two hundred thousand dollars was a ton of

hush money.

"Did it work? Did she back off and keep quiet?"

"There was one more incident on set. She bought a Porsche like mine. Our cars were identical. A new security guard let her on the lot. Keith spotted her before she got to me and they escorted her off the premises. After that I filed a restraining order and she stayed away."

"You should've seen the look on Keith's face when he saw her walking down the street."

"I'm not surprised. He's the only person who knew what was going on. I could trust him more than I could trust myself. After Gisela and Jackie, I couldn't let anyone in. I didn't want to make any more mistakes. It was one of the reasons I agreed to the fake relationship with Eden. It was the only kind of relationship I thought I was capable of." He paused and captured my gaze. "Until I met you. You changed everything."

Derek's faith in me was astonishing. He opened up and freely gave me his trust. Now there weren't any more secrets. We were free from our past.

"Derek, I love you."

He hurried to my side and gathered me in his arms. "I love you too. You're everything, you and Molly. You're my family. I can't lose you."

"You won't, I'm so stubborn I won't let you."

The rigid strain in Derek's shoulders waned. His lips delivered featherlight kisses on my cheeks, nose, and forehead. His eyes wandered to the bandage on my head. He touched it tenderly with his fingertips. "Does it hurt?"

"It's much better now. You're like magic."

He smiled. "I'm going to bring you something to eat and then I want you to rest. I can't wait to hold you all night."

He gave me a gentle peck and rose to his feet. Before he left the room, I remembered something about my eerie interaction with Jackie.

"By the way, do you have a Lamborghini?"

"Yeah, why?"

"Thank God, because Jackie asked Keith if the Porsche was still the only car you let anyone drive, and I lied and said, I drove all of your cars including your Lamborghini."

He teased. "Well, I might have to think about that, young lady."

We chuckled a bit. Then it hit me. I whispered the word Porsche repeatedly until the fog lifted in my brain. "Oh, my God."

"Sweetie, what is it?"

My breath lodged in my throat. "Your car, your Porsche was parked outside the restaurant. Jackie saw it and said she still had her Porsche. When I made the comment about the Lamborghini, I said I was driving us home. I didn't see the car that hit us, but there was this man. He helped me. He told me he saw the whole thing. Now I remember. He said, 'That Porsche came out of nowhere.' It was Jackie. I know it. She thought I was driving. This was no accident. She tried to kill me."

Frantic, I searched for my purse determined to call the officers.

"Nia, what are doing?"

"I'm calling the police."

He placed a firm grip on my shoulders. "Don't. We're not positive it was her. This needs to be handled delicately. I can't risk rattling her cage."

I raised my voice in disbelief. "You have got to be kidding me. Your best friend is in a hospital bed and you want to handle things delicately? Don't you get it? I said I was driving home. It should've been me. It's my fault. Keith could've been killed. I have to do something."

"Listen to me. This is not your fight. It's mine. If you're right and Jackie did this, I'm the reason Keith is in that bed, not you. Give me twenty-four hours to figure out something. Then you can call the police. Get back in bed, now."

I scampered to the bed like a scolded child, but I wasn't about to let this go.

"Tomorrow I'm going to the hospital to visit Keith and then I'm flying back to Vegas. When your twenty-four hours are up, I'm calling the police. I'm doing the right thing. What are you going to do?"

# Chapter Ten

At the end of the day, Derek did the right thing. There was something to be said for handling the situation delicately. He hired a private investigator and they tracked down Jackie's car at a body shop in Hollywood Hills. The damage on the front end was a dead giveaway. Officer Belly and Baldy arrested her and took her to the station for questioning. She confessed to hit-and-run, but claimed it was an accident. After being processed, Belly uncovered something Derek didn't know about her. Jackie was Canadian and her Visa expired a year ago. She was promptly deported.

Two weeks passed and Derek was busier than ever in LA. He worked like a dog promoting *Traitors in Our Midst.* The film opened with little fanfare and solid reviews. I missed Vegas Derek terribly. LA Derek remained steadfast in his distracted, short-tempered ways. I reverted to my old habits and quit answering my phone. It only added to the stress of our relationship and created more tension.

One scorching hot day in July, I experienced the day from hell. Shannon and Lacey had a blow up. Lacey cracked a few too many unflattering barbs about Walter, and Shannon let her have it. She had a major crush on Walter, even after he left Steve and Scott's going away party with the stilt walker.

I consulted with Brooke and she suggested I do all the private spin classes with Walter. Unfortunately, it made sense. If Lacey didn't engage with Walter, perhaps she would keep her inappropriate yet hilarious comments to herself.

I powered through a class with Walter and ran home to change and pick up Molly. The two of us cruised back to my office and got to work. I calculated payroll, while Molly destroyed her new toy hot dog.

I glanced up and found Walter in my office. "Oh, hey, did you need something?"

He helped himself to a chair. "No, I just wanted to say thanks for the class today. It was great. Oh, and I wanted to see how you're feeling. Shannon said you were in a car accident when you were in LA a few weeks ago."

Note to self, stop telling Shannon my personal business. We managed to keep the accident out of the press. I sidestepped the issue. "It was just a fender bender. I'm fine."

"Good to know. We can't let anything happen to my favorite instructor."

*Holy shit!* Is Walter flirting with me? What did Shannon see in him?

Speaking of which, Shannon popped her head around the door. She wasn't pleased to see the object of her affection chatting me up.

In an abrupt tone she said, "Nia, you have a call on line two."

Thank God! Normally I'd asked who it was, but I didn't care. Talk about being saved by the bell. Once the "happy couple" was out of my office I took the call.

"This is Nia, can I help you?"

There was a long deliberate pause followed by a haunting, familiar voice, a voice from my past that straightened my spine.

The pinched tone on the other end of the phone said, "Hello, it's Evelyn. How are you?"

Evelyn Michaels, my stepmother. The woman who made my life a living hell after my mom died. Granted, she sent my inheritance from my dad. It was the only decent thing she'd ever done. I wrote to say thank you and told her about Sammy's Place, the charity Dad's money funded. There was zero point to any further communication.

The hairs on the back of my neck rose as I icily responded. "I'm fine. What do you want?"

Evelyn spoke in her sweet, fake ass voice. Growing up I called it the danger tone. It couldn't be trusted. "Oh, don't be silly. I don't want a thing. Can't a woman call her stepdaughter and say congratulations on your engagement? The girls and I saw your picture in a magazine. We're so happy for you."

A small smug part of me reaped a bit of satisfaction knowing step-mommy dearest and her two brats, Natalie and Ashley, ate their hearts out when they saw pictures of me with my dashing fiancé. I envisioned the three over-processed blondes with their acrylic nails and matching Hello Kitty ensembles, disgusted and envious as they scrutinized every photo. The one thing they weren't was happy for me.

Evelyn prattled on. "The girls watch your fiancé on his vampire show. They think he is the dreamiest thing. Have you set a date? If you need anything just let me know."

And there it was, the real reason she called. It wasn't about me. It was about my famous fiancé.

The angry teenager within bubbled out. "I don't need anything from you. I never have."

The real Evelyn appeared with a vengeance. She was a total bitch, but at least she was honest. "You listen here, *Meagan,* your father would roll over in his grave if he heard the way you talked to me. You are the same disrespectful, hateful child you always were."

I could've torn her to shreds. Lord knows I had enough ammunition. Instead, a light bulb went off. I stayed strong, determined to rid her from my life for good.

"Evelyn, my dad would be disappointed in both of us. After all these years, I've finally figured out why you hate me so much. You can't manipulate me and it drives you crazy."

Her defensiveness reached fever pitch. "That's not true. I don't hate you and I most certainly don't manipulate anyone."

"Jesus, just freaking own it. You don't like me and I don't like you. It's fine. Believe it or not, I wish you well, but we're done. Don't call me again."

The line went dead. She hung up. Tears threatened my eyes, but I wasn't going to cry over her. I sat on the floor with Molly and she immediately brought a smile to my face. Payroll beckoned, so I got back to work, convinced the day could only improve from here.

Lacey trounced in my office with a of look displeasure. She shut the door and slouched into a chair.

"Am I being fired?" she asked.

"No, why would you think that?"

"Shannon said from now on you're teaching Walter's private spin classes?"

Damn it, Shannon needs to shut it. "I am, but I was going to give you someone else. I know you don't like him."

"Do you like him?"

"Just between us, he creeps me out too. But Shannon has a crush on him, so we need to keep our opinions to ourselves."

Lacey saluted me. "Okay, chief. Message received loud and clear."

Without knocking, Shannon burst through the door. "Oh, sorry, am I interrupting?"

Lacey shot back, "No, and Nia's not firing me, if that's what you're hoping."

"Geez, what is with you? I can't believe you said that. I was actually looking for you. Christa, the new spin instructor, didn't show for Sharon Gill's private class. Can you do it?"

"Heck, yeah, I'm a team player, I guess not everyone is."

She pushed her way past Shannon in a huff. Before Shannon left, I motioned for her to come in and take a seat.

"I don't know what's going on between you and Lacey, but you two need to work it out."

"Did you say the same thing to her?"

"Yes, I did. Also, the woman that called me earlier, her name is Evelyn Michaels. She's my stepmother. Don't ever put her through to me again. And please don't tell anyone about it. Just assume everything I say is confidential."

An expression of hurt crossed Shannon's face. "I would never say anything. You can trust me, Nia."

"Okay, just be sure to always ask who's calling, so I'm not caught off guard again."

Shannon shoved out of the chair in a dramatic fashion. "I will. I guess I can't do anything right today."

After Shannon exited, I looked at Molly and said, "Is there a PMS summit that we don't know about?"

I had to get out of there.

* * * *

I rifled through the mail at home. My day finally perked up when I spotted a card from Derek. It was romantic card with gold lettering and frayed edges. The verse on the inside was standard poetic fare. What turned me into lovey-dovey goo was Derek's handwritten words.

My angel, I miss holding you and kissing you good night.

I miss waking up with you and kissing you good morning.

I miss you. I miss us.

Maybe a glimpse of Vegas Derek crept into LA Derek. My heart beamed after I read it. God, I missed him too. I should call him and tell him how much I loved him. We hadn't talked in three days. Just hearing his voice would do me a world of good.

Before I grabbed my phone, I spied an official looking letter. *Oh no!* My hands shook. It was a subpoena. Nick's parents were suing Metro, claiming wrongful death. I had to give a deposition. I sank to the kitchen floor with my head in my hands. I'd be face-to-face with Nick's mom and dad, the people who despised me the most. That horrific night came screaming back. The way Nick clawed at my dress and beat me. I could see the gun pointed at us in those final terrifying moments. It left me immobile. I curled into the fetal position and wept on the kitchen floor.

I glanced up when I heard footsteps. He was there. It was Derek.

I wiped my eyes and squeaked out, "Hi."

He knelt down and drew me into his arms, cloaking me in love.

Through my tears, I choked, "You're here."

His voice was sweet and soft. "Of course I'm here."

My body folded into his. I couldn't curb the never-ending stream of tears.

"Shhh…don't cry, my sweet girl. It's going to be okay. I left LA as soon as I found out about the deposition. We'll get through this together. You're not alone."

Derek removed the tear-stained subpoena clutched in my hands. He scooped me up and carried me to our bedroom. The entire way he comforted me, making my tears subside. He placed me on the bed and went to the bathroom. The absence of his touch threatened a fresh wave of sobs.

He appeared with a washcloth, noticing the return of my involuntary tears. "Hey, you know it's going to be okay, right?"

"I do. I just didn't want you to let me go."

He sat on the bed and held me on his lap. "I'm never letting go. In fact, I'm going to be in Vegas so much, you'll be sick of me."

It was like music to my ears. Derek soothed me, dabbing the cool washcloth on my face. We cuddled up in bed. My head was on his chest, and his beautiful hands stroked my back. Vegas Derek was here. The stress of the day and tension of the past weeks extinguished and replaced with a serene calm. Yes, everything would be okay.

I was so peaceful. I'd almost forgotten. "My stepmother called me today."

"She did?"

"Yep, how's that for a lousy day, a call from step-mommy dearest and a subpoena."

"You've always said your stepmother hated you and made your life miserable, but you never said why."

"I think it would be easier to show you."

I padded across the floor and grabbed my mom's jewelry box. The small cherry wood box housed the gorgeous emerald earrings and diamond crusted cuff that Derek bought me. However, the real reason it was so special was my mom's locket and the pictures my dad sent me.

I showed him my favorite photo of Mom and me. Granted, it was one of those Sears Portrait studio pictures, but I treasured it.

Derek gasped. "Oh, my God, you look exactly like your mom. She was beautiful, just like you."

"I didn't realize it at the time, but now I get it. I was a living reminder of the only woman my dad would ever love. As much as my stepmom liked to pretend, deep down, I think she knew.

"One time, Dad took us on vacation. I was fourteen. My stepsister, Natalie was ten, and Ashley was only seven. We had adjoining rooms. Evelyn just scolded me. I asked for money for the vending machine. I had a hankering for *Sun Chips*. If I wanted something, the response from my stepmom was always the same. 'You don't need that. Wants and needs are two different things.' I went back to our room and took a nap. When I woke up, the adjoining door was open a little. I peeked in and there was Natalie and Ashley munching down on *Sun Chips*. They were playing Go Fish. Ashley was nestled on my dad's lap. He didn't see me, but my stepmother did. With a calculated lilt in her step, she shut the door in my face."

"Sweetie, I'm so sorry."

"It was like she was telling me you're not welcome. You don't belong. The truth is I didn't. It hit me today when I was talking to her. She hated me, because she couldn't manipulate me like everyone else. It was a vicious cycle. I'd call her out on her bullshit, she would go to my dad and then I'd be the bad guy. I wanted to belong, but I didn't."

Derek pressed his lips to mine.

"Baby, you do belong. You belong to me. You are mine and I am yours. We belong together."

# Chapter Eleven

I did belong to Derek. The following week we were inseparable. Our connection and love thrived. Unfortunately, he had to venture back to LA. His vampire character on *First Bite*, Drake Braden, was gaining a new love interest. A casting call went out and Derek auditioned all the potential actresses. I didn't relish the idea of my fiancé and tons of gorgeous women in a room together. But when Derek sent me an entire crate of *Sun Chips* the day after he left, I didn't give them a second thought.

Things turned back to normal at work too. After a couple of Tequila shots at Brooke's house, Lacey and Shannon forgot about their argument. It was quite the drunken gabfest with all my girls. Everyone turned it up, but me. It was vital to be home early and sober for Derek's phone call.

The past couple of nights we partook in something new and naughty, phone sex. It was the next best thing to being there. We set a date for nine p.m. I left Brooke's house at eight-thirty.

I freshened myself up for Derek even though he wouldn't actually be here. At nine o'clock on the dot, my cell rang. Filthy shenanigans were about to commence.

In a breathy voice I answered, "Hi."

Derek wasted zero time getting after it. "What are you wearing?"

"I'm naked."

His voice was hushed and sexy. "Are you wet for me?"

I whispered, "Yes."

Even over the phone, Derek was in charge. "Slide your hand down you body, dip a finger inside, tell me how it feels."

"It feels good. I'm such a bad girl. I'm pleasuring myself without you."

"What did I say I would do if I caught you starting without me?"

"You would make me finish without you."

"Good girl," he uttered in such a faint voice I could barely hear him. "Put two fingers inside and pump my beautiful pussy."

I obeyed and squirmed under the power of my own hand. My moans escalated, growing louder with each thrust.

Derek's voice piped in, clear as a bell, "Yes, baby. Don't hold back. Let me hear you."

My middle finger was just long enough to press on my sweet spot. I cried out and dropped the phone. Scrambling to retrieve it, I lifted my head…and gasped.

*Son of bitch!* Derek was here, wearing nothing but a provocative, dirty grin and an enormous mouth watering erection.

I shrieked, "Oh, my God! What are you doing here?"

He sauntered to me. "I think the question is what are you doing?"

His fingertips danced on his lips. I found him adorable, hot and a total schemer.

I batted my eyes at him. "Well, my fiancé told me to pump his beautiful pussy. I did what I was told. Shouldn't I get some sort of lick my greedy cunt reward?"

He delighted in our little game. "I'm afraid we had a deal. If I caught you starting without me, I would watch you finish without me."

*Holy shit!* He was serious, and positioned himself between my thighs.

"But you tricked me and… Uh…"

He opened my legs. "Nia, look at me. You are so unbelievably sexy. I'm going to watch you make yourself come and then I'm going to fuck some of that naughty out of you. Understand?"

I swallowed hard and nodded. I could do this. I wanted to do this. His penetrating stare was so inviting, I slid my hand down to my sex.

The corners of his mouth upturned in a decadent smile. "Good girl. Spread yourself open. Let me see your pink."

Completely turned on and obedient I widened my lips and explored my glistening billows of lust. I arched my back and closed my eyes, giving into this torrid pleasure.

"Look at me, baby, give me your eyes."

His eyes met mine, searing me into a seductive trance.

"Feel how wet you are. God I love it." Derek couldn't contain himself. A dollop of pre-cum escaped from his tip and he stroked his straining erection, heightening our arousal. I plunged two fingers inside, pushing myself to the crest.

Derek groaned, "That's it, fuck my sweet cunt."

I convulsed and cried out while I continued my assault. My other hand circled my ready clit until I burst before his wicked glare. I felt so free in my bold prowess.

As my breathless state returned to normal, he palmed my hipbones and kissed my belly button. "Amazing."

My desire for him conjured up images of my mouth sheathed around him. I could be like a one-woman coming machine.

"Speaking of amazing, that is one gigantic situation you have there. I'd like take care of that for you."

He was flat on his back in less than a second. "Well, if you insist."

"I insist!"

Derek's regal erect column was an embarrassment of riches. His crown was kingly. I worshiped it properly with my tongue as any good subject would. My rimming skills elated his scepter and rewarded me with absolute hardness.

I immersed my dutiful mouth on him and he groaned and twitched. I baptized his royal staff with an exalted sheen of wetness. My hands joined the festivities, delighting his shaft in a tantric twist. Then I helped myself to a lusty throat full of cock. His tip stormed the gate of my tonsils. He grabbed fistfuls of my hair, while I guzzled him into a steady rhythm of deep throaty delirium.

His body tensed under the strain of his inevitable release. "Jesus, fuck…ah…fucking amazing."

I eased off his mighty wand with my eyes watering and spit dripping down my chin, leaving him coated in a hefty supply of my saliva. My hands and mouth pleased him in concert. I tasted the succulent elixir of his silky pre-cum. He gripped my head, convulsing on the bed. I ruled him mightily with an honorable shafting of his noble sword. With another battery of devoted, deep guzzling mouth strokes, my king came off his throne and his delectable nectar christened my throat.

I cherished every drop he bequeathed me, licking him clean like a faithful, mouth and handmaiden. My lips curtsied to his balls and delivered reverent kisses and lusty licks. As the flat of my tongue glided up his weapon of mass destruction, he swelled with blustery power, and was ready for battle again. Maybe I was amazing.

I would've been joyful to bestow my mouth on him all night, but Derek said, "Come here, sweetie."

I flopped on the bed next to him, so proud of myself. I'd driven both of us to the heights of pleasure, and Derek's cock was still hard as a rock. He wasted no time making good on his promise to fuck the naughty out of me. He reached into the nightstand and grabbed the bottle of lube. *Oh, shit!* What was he up to?

He must've seen my eyes grow to the size of his erection. "Baby, relax. I know you're not ready for me yet. But, maybe we could try something. Do you trust me?"

The bad girl inside me was intrigued. "Butt, of course."

He positioned me between his legs, my back to his front. Somehow, he made the technical aspects of his finger in my bunghole sound sexy. He swept my dark hair to the side and said softly. "In the past when I put my finger in there, I only used the tip of my index finger, tonight I want to push you a little further. I want to fill you more."

I nodded yes and nestled into his chest. He pressed his lips to my temple and I lifted my chin so he could take my mouth. He lavished me with deep sultry tongue kisses that vibrated to my creamy center. Our bodies heaved in hunger for one another. He skimmed his fingers over my breasts, past my torso and inside my ready pussy. Derek let out a benevolent groan when he felt how I dripped for him. Both of his hands went to my hips, gently maneuvering me into place. I was on all fours facing away from him, burning with anticipation.

I speared myself with his robust cock, grinding with unrestrained enthusiasm. Yes, I didn't just want this. I craved it. I needed him to fill me. I felt daring in my wanton state of savage lust. Yearning for more I rode him like a fiend as an orgasm lurked within.

Derek quieted our pace. "Are you ready, sweetie?"

"Yes, please. Oh God, yes."

I heard the bottle of lube click open, then a moment of silence as my internal muscles clenched. Derek spread my cheeks and a dollop of lube touched my entrance. I held my breath and tensed.

His calming hands caressed my behind. "Just breathe, baby."

I released a long shaky breath and my body relaxed.

"Good girl. Let me know if it's too much. I don't want to hurt you."

I panted. "Okay. I'm ready."

Derek's finger proceeded forth into my tight, dark channel. The welcome intruder eased in and out slowly, allowing my body to accommodate the fullness of Derek's cock and his finger buried to his knuckle.

He whispered, "So good. Now, touch yourself. I want you to feel it all."

The sawing of my ass, the pumping of my pussy, and the kneading of my clit, fueled an inferno. I was being fucked three ways to Sunday. He took me on a sinful journey to another dimension. A great pressure howled within. Derek re-lubed and pummeled my ass with his dedicated digit. My pussy wept on his cock, anointing him with my cum. One orgasm after another seized my body.

I screamed his name. I didn't know how much more I could take.

He growled. "That's it. Give me everything. Fuck, yes."

One quick slap on my ass launched us over the rim to grunting, wailing cries of indulgent debauchery. We trembled, milking our mutual climax to its diabolical conclusion. He snaked his arm around my waist bringing me next to him. Our bodies shivered in rich repletion.

His lips found mine and delivered a tender kiss. "Nia, you're perfection."

I smiled back. "Are you sure about that? I think there's some naughty left that you didn't fuck out."

He held me close. "Exactly, perfection."

# Chapter Twelve

Two days later, we woke to our moment of dread. It was the day of the deposition. We'd be face-to-face with Nick's parents.

I opened my eyes to find Derek wide-awake, wearing a strained expression. It pained me to see him like that, especially since this was my fault. We still suffered the wounds from my past. There was also another secret, Nick's ring. It was in Julia's guesthouse in one of her dresser drawers. I should've told him about it months ago, but I didn't. I couldn't step foot in the guesthouse after Nick's attack. Now I had no choice. Despite everything, it was imperative I returned their family heirloom.

When my sleepy eyes met Derek's he pasted on a smile for my benefit. "Good morning, my sweet girl."

I responded quietly, "Hi."

His lips brushed my forehead and I tensed. "Hey, you know everything is going be okay. Facing Nick's parents will be tough, but we'll get through it, together."

I stammered, "I–I k–know. I–I have something to tell you. Something I–I should've told you a long time ago."

"You know you can tell me anything."

"I–I still have Nick's wedding ring. I would've thrown it away ages ago, but it doesn't belong to me. It belongs to his family. I–I need to give back to them."

"Okay, that's fine. Is that all?"

"The ring is in Julia's guesthouse. I got upset one night and threw it in one of the dresser drawers. I haven't been there since…"

"Oh, my angel, come here. I'll go get the ring. I don't want you to go back there, ever. Don't worry about a thing. Today we will close this chapter for good. They can't hurt you anymore. I promise."

* * * *

Derek and I sat motionless in the back seat of his large, black car. Jake Malone, our new regular Las Vegas driver, cranked the air conditioner full blast, as we idled outside of Cammie Lester and Associates' office. I was grateful the deposition took place at the court reporter's office and not the courthouse downtown. This was more private. It was only the discovery phase of the case. Hopefully, they'd discover Nick's parents had no case.

Derek's thumb grazed my knuckles. I held on to his hand so tight our palms sweated. It was time. We had to get out of the car. Derek motioned to Jake and he promptly opened my door. The blistering Vegas heat smacked me in the face as I steadied myself on the sidewalk. Derek began ushering me inside when a limo appeared curbside. My mouth went dry. It was Richard and Judy Ryan, Nick's parents. I stopped dead in my tracks when they spied me. My heart raced so fast my head dizzied. They threw me a familiar look, disdain mixed with disgust. Even though Richard and Judy were small in stature, they possessed an intimidating presence. Before they walked inside, the limo window opened. Judy turned and said something to whoever was inside. I recognized the stock Ryan family finger wag.

We held back and allowed them to enter the building first. The tinted windows of the limo prevented me from eyeing who was inside. Perhaps it was one of Nick's brothers.

Inside, Derek's lawyer, Martin Dinkel greeted us. Today he acted as my lawyer too. He was tall like Derek, and resembled a thin Mr. Clean. He introduced us to Cammie Lester. Her pretty, green eyes lit up when she shook Derek's hand. What a surprise, she personally handled our case. We followed Cammie to a room with a large conference table and no windows. Richard and Judy sat with their lawyer. Officer Mendez and Grayson addressed us warmly as they introduced their counsel, Mark King.

Sweat trickled down my back. My head throbbed in this tension-filled room. Why were we even here? They had no case against the officers. Derek was an eyewitness. This was personal. They wanted to see me suffer, just like their son. I unintentionally granted them their wish. My emotions overwhelmed me when I delivered my deposition. Richard and Judy glared in disbelief. They mocked me, as if I was a child spinning a tale. I clutched Derek's hand for strength. He never let go.

Before Derek spoke, Richard and Judy's lawyer interrupted. Bob Singer was a smarmy, ridiculous zit of a human being. His nasal tone combined with a thick Pittsburgh accent made his lies even more unbearable. "My clients believe Mr. Pierce's eyewitness testimony is a lie. He corroborated the officers' account because he wanted Nick Ryan dead.

"The fact is, we really don't know who fired their weapon first. I submit, Nick Ryan acted in self-defense and wasn't a threat to anyone. He only wanted his wife back. His wife and her lover wanted Nick out of the way. There isn't a shred of evidence to prove Nick meant Miss Kelly, well actually Mrs. Ryan, any harm. It's only her word against a dead man. A dead man Metro police killed in cold blood."

Derek's grip on my hand tightened. I was surprised he didn't leap across the table and strangle Bob.

Mark King, shot up from his chair. "Actually we have plenty of proof." He slid a photo of me to the Ryan's and Bob from the night of the attack. I shielded my face. I couldn't look.

Bob was unfazed. "This doesn't mean anything. It could be photoshopped or whatnot."

Mark fired back, "It is official evidence collected

on April 28. I have over a dozen statements from paramedics and other officers. Oh, and I just received these transcripts. Larry Wall turned over every correspondence with the deceased. It further proves Nick was the mastermind, and his intention was to find Miss Kelly and kill her. Mr. and Mrs. Ryan, I'm sorry you lost your son, but you have no case."

Mark handed Bob the transcripts. Upon further examination, Bob looked at Richard and Judy, shaking his head. Richard slammed his fist against the table.

Judy wept. "My son." She collected herself, and wagged her bony finger at me with cold, dark eyes. "You did this. You drove him to it. One day he comes and tells us you're pregnant and then you vanished into thin air."

My entire body shook. Her venomous stare looked just like Nick's as she continued her rant. "Nick went crazy trying to find you. And you just sit there with your expensive ring and new fiancé like it's nothing. You make me sick."

Derek flew up from his seat. "Enough!"

Martin muttered. "Derek, don't."

He exhaled and reached in his pocket, producing the ring, the Ryan family heirloom. He placed it on the table. "Nia wanted to give this back to you. We don't want any trouble. We just want to be left alone."

Richard picked up the ring and said to me, "You think this makes up for what you did to my son? It means nothing. Maybe you didn't fire the gun, but you killed him just the same. May you never have another minute of peace, murderer."

"Shut up!" It popped out of my mouth with zero control. "Just shut up!" Everyone jerked their heads to me. My jaw quivered, but I stood, squared my shoulders and spoke the truth. "Your son beat me. Your son punched me when I was pregnant. Your son nearly killed me. I'm glad he's dead." Richard and Judy gasped in horror. "It was either going to be him or me. If only one of us could come out alive, I'm glad it was me. Your son was a monster."

The room erupted in chaos. Judy lunged over the table with fists flying. Derek blocked her from me, and Grayson and Mendez jolted out of their seats ready to protect us. That only fueled Richard and Judy's fury. Stuck with trying to hold them back, Bob winced when a random elbow socked him in the gut.

Derek shouted, "Stop. It's over. Everybody stop. This is over."

Richard calmed, but Judy continued flailing. "It's not over. It's never going to be over."

A shell-shocked Cammie opened the door. "Mr. Singer, will you please show your clients off the premises."

Bob nodded. "There's nothing more we can do. I'm sorry. We should go."

The last thing I expected was Bob Singer to be the voice of reason. He escorted them out, but not before Judy pinned me with a hateful stare and spit on the floor.

When the door shut behind them, I fell into Derek's arms.

He whispered in my ear, "I'm proud of you for standing up to them."

I peered up at him. "Only because you were by my side."

He smiled. "Always."

Officers Grayson and Mendez said their goodbyes, but Martin and Mark remained locked in an intense conversation. Martin made a gesture to Derek.

Derek nodded and said to me, "I need to talk to Martin for a minute. Let's get you in the car. I'll make sure Jake stays with you."

I settled in the back seat. Julia, Brooke, Shannon, and Lacey blew up my phone. They were curious about the deposition. By the time I answered all their messages, Derek climbed in the car with the weight of the world still on his shoulders.

"Honey, what's wrong?"

Derek released a heavy sigh. "Larry Wall's going to get out of jail soon."

"What?"

"He struck a deal when he turned over all his correspondences with Nick. It made the case against Metro go away, but it also lessened his sentence."

My eyes were wide with fear. "He's going to come after me, I know it."

Derek grasped my hands. "He won't. I won't let

him."

"I can't believe this. This isn't right. Don't they know he'll leave jail and head straight for Las Vegas?"

"His parole hearing is in September and if he's released, he'll still be on probation. He won't be able to leave California."

This was preposterous. Today I finally put Nick and his family behind me only to have a new threat beating down my door. When was it going to end?

I rested my head on Derek's shoulder. It was only three in the afternoon, but I was exhausted.

He smoothed my hair. "Martin asked if I could meet with him today. I'm going to drop you off at home and have Jake take me to his office. I promise it won't take long."

"You can't do it another time?"

"No, I'm sorry, sweetie. I should only be gone a half hour at the most. After that I'm all yours."

I conceded and nestled back on Derek's shoulder. My phone vibrated with a text. It was Shannon, asking if I was going to the club or going home. I texted back and said Derek was dropping me off at home and going to a meeting. She offered to drive down to the security gates and pick me up. I took her up on her offer. The sooner Derek met with Martin the sooner he'd be home with me.

As we approached the gates, I spotted Walter James leaving the security booth laughing his head off. He sauntered over to Shannon's car. She rolled down her window, and it looked like he helped himself to a kiss. *What the heck?*

Derek gave me a gentle peck. I scooted out of the car and hopped into Shannon's blue Toyota. I exchanged an awkward greeting with Walter before he jumped in his golf cart and left. I intended on pressing Shannon about the smooch, but she beat me to the punch. "So, tell me how it went? Did you see Nick's parents?"

Shannon was privy to everything about Nick and Larry. Right after I hired her, we spent a wine-soaked evening at my place swapping stories. After all, she came on board at the country club right after the incident with Nick and had Sonya's old job. It was only natural for her to be curious.

I coughed up a blow-by-blow account of the day while Shannon drove me home.

"Do you want some company? I could stay with you until Derek gets back?"

"That's okay. You don't need to babysit me. I'll be fine. I'm going to do a couple of things around the house and then go for a swim."

"Swim? I didn't think you knew how to swim?"

"Derek taught me a couple of weeks ago. I mean, I'm not very good. But I like it."

"Oh, okay. Call me if you need anything."

As soon as I walked in the house I received an enthusiastic welcome from little Molly. I gathered her up only to realize she wasn't so little anymore. Our puppy packed on a good eight pounds since we adopted her. What was it about the unconditional love of a dog? I found it to be one of life's magical charms.

I fed my hungry pooch and she trotted out the doggie door. After checking the mail and straightening up the kitchen, I went upstairs to change. A dip in the pool was just what I needed to wash this day away. I gladly removed my black dress and donned a bikini.

When I landed in the kitchen, my heart skipped a beat. The back door leading to the patio was open. "Derek," I called for him. Maybe he came home and was outside with Molly. "Molly, Derek," I said a little louder and stepped out onto the patio.

*Good God, no!* It was Melissa! Melissa Baker, Nick's mistress, was in my backyard, clutching Molly by the throat, dangling her over the pool. A blind rage flashed through me and a cry ripped from my throat.

I hurled myself fast as lightening to rescue Molly, screaming, "Let her go!"

I tackled Melissa and we crashed into the pool. Molly yelped. When I broke free and swam to the surface, Molly paddled her way to safety. Before I reached her, Melissa wrenched my neck in a choke hold, and shoved me under water. She cursed me as I clawed to wriggle away. Melissa had four inches and thirty pounds on me, but there was no fucking way she would take me down. With the edge of the pool in sight, I escaped her clutches. Hoisting myself nearly free, Melissa latched onto my ankle. With all my might,

I shook her off and turned to face her. Her eyes raged with delirious hatred as she sputtered to climb out of the pool.

I stared her down. "Get out of my house!"

My foot clocked her right in the face. I kicked her so hard blood flew in the air and she fell back in the water. I scooped up Molly and ran back to the house at breakneck speed.

*The phone. I need my phone. I have to call 911. Damn it, where is my fucking phone?*

I sat Molly down and rummaged through my purse. "Come on. Come on. Where is it?"

*Oh, fuck!* Melissa rose out of the water with a newfound determination. My shaking hand plucked up my phone. "Come on, Molly." I picked her up and sped out the front door. Melissa wasn't far behind. I screamed for help while I dialed. Suddenly my phone spiraled through the air and smashed onto the sidewalk.

I spun around, and Melissa seethed, "What's it going to be, you or the dog?" The words spilled out of her mouth in a quiet, maniacal tone. "I was going to kill the mutt. Seemed only fair after you took someone I loved, but then you went and kicked me in the face, so now I can't decide."

"Melissa, there has been enough pain, and enough loss. It has to end. Look what it's doing to you."

The woman before me was broken. I used to see her as a beast, the strong, buxom blonde who had a hold on Nick. Now she was a shell of a person.

Tears sprung in her eyes. "He was almost over you, you know. He started to forget about you. I did that. Nick and me could've had a life together. Then that guy, Larry calls, says he knows where you are. His obsession with you started all over again. I told him to forget about you and think about his family, me and the baby."

I sat Molly on the ground, in shock. "The baby? What baby?"

Melissa dropped her guard. "Our baby, a son, Nicky."

Nick had a son. With tentative steps, I walked to her in sympathy. "Melissa, I'm sorry. I never wanted any of this. I wanted Nick to move on and forget all about me. I'm so sorry."

Anger filled her eyes. "You're sorry? That's all you have to say to me? My baby's going to grow up without his father, and you're sorry?"

In one rapid motion, she trounced me to the ground. With my arms pinned under hers, she shouted in my face. "It's your fault. It's your fault he's dead."

A car screeched to a halt. Melissa kneed my chest, cutting off my air. In a flash, Derek ripped her off me, holding her down.

He tossed me his phone. "Call 911."

I looked at Melissa on the ground drowning in agony. I couldn't do it.

"Nia, I said call 911."

"No, it's Melissa. She has a baby, Nick's baby. I

can't take his mother away from him. Derek, let her go."

Melissa sobbed. "Please, let me go. I won't hurt anyone, I swear it."

Cautiously Derek released her. I extended my hand. "Melissa, no more. Go home. Go home to your son."

She placed her hand in mine and stood up. "You really ain't going to call the police? You're not going to press charges?"

I glanced at Derek and swallowed hard. "No, we aren't. But in exchange, you and Nick's family have to leave us alone or the deal is off."

A black limo raced down our street and ground to a sharp stop right in front of our house. It was Nick's parents. How did they know where I lived? How in the hell did they get past security? Jake asserted a protective posture on the sidewalk.

I looked Melissa directly in the eyes. "I mean it. If any of you bother us again, you'll go to jail for a very long time. Do the right thing. Do it for your son."

Nick's parents jumped out of the limo screaming at Melissa to get in the car. Her head darted back and forth.

"You have my word." Melissa said. "You'll never hear from any of us again."

Jake thwarted the Ryan's attempt to charge us.

Melissa searched my face, as if she was trying to tell me something. "Melissa, what is it? Tell me."

Nick's mom screeched, "Melissa, don't you dare

say a word. Get in the car."

Melissa mouthed, "I'm sorry" and left. The limo zoomed away. I took one look at Derek and folded into him.

He held me tighter than ever before. "Oh, my baby. When we pulled up, I thought the worst. God, if anything ever happens to you."

Jake interrupted, "Mr. Pierce, would you like me stay awhile?"

"Yeah, that would be a good idea." Derek turned his attention back to me. "Sweetie, are you sure you're okay? Do want to go to the hospital and get checked out?"

"No, I'm fine. Molly. Where's Molly?" I found her cowered under the tree. "Derek, she's shaking. Can you help me?"

He gingerly gathered her up in his arms. "What the hell happened?"

I kissed my puppy's head. "Melissa had her by throat, she came to kill her."

"How the fuck did they know we have dog or where we live?"

"I don't know. It doesn't make any sense."

"Tomorrow I'm going to talk to security."

And by talk, Derek meant rip someone a new one. He would do anything to protect us.

A sudden realization touched my heart. This man, my beautiful fiancé not only swept me away with his love, he saved me today, more than once.

I stood on my tiptoes and kissed his cheek. "Thank you."

"Thank me? Thank me for what?"

"Thank you for saving our lives today."

"Sweetie, I didn't do anything. I should've never left your side today. When I think about what could've happened."

"Derek you don't understand. Melissa thought I didn't know how to swim. Nick embarrassed me at a company picnic one year. He told everyone I couldn't swim. But I can, because you taught me. Your love allowed me to open up and face my fears. You saved me. You saved us."

With Molly cradled in his arms he pressed his lips to mine. "And now I'm going to take care of my girls. Come. Let's get you both a bath."

We padded across the lawn toward the house. "By the way, I noticed Melissa was bleeding, but you don't really have a scratch on you."

"I kicked here a good one, right in the face."

"That's my girl."

# Chapter Thirteen

The next day Jake drove us to the police station to file a report. Even if we weren't pressing charges, Derek wasn't taking any chances. We also got a restraining order on Nick's family and Larry Wall.

Then Derek and Brooke marched to the head of security at the Mountain Heights Country Club. Brooke fired the guards on duty yesterday and demanded more thorough background checks for all new hires.

Under Jake's watchful eye, I enjoyed a cuddle on the floor with Molly at home. As I suspected he was both driver and bodyguard. I suppose it could be worse. Jake was hot in a biker dude kind of way. He wasn't really my type, although he did fill out his sensible trousers quite nicely.

The bell rang, it was my trusty assistant Lacey with a new phone for me. She said she had to dash off, so I quickly introduced her to Jake. Suddenly she wasn't in such a hurry and joined me for a glass of wine. I offered a glass to Jake. He politely declined with a trace of a smile. Perhaps I made a match.

Derek returned home, and within an hour, our entire gang flocked to our house for an impromptu barbeque. This was exactly what I needed after yesterday—Derek, Molly, and I surrounded by good food, good friends, and lots of love. I belonged.

* * * *

Derek climbed in bed that night wearing nothing but an adorable grin. God, I think he could make me come with one look. My entire being was linked to every cell in his body.

I asked, "What's that look for?"

"Well, I'm afraid I was cornered by every one of your girlfriends tonight. They wanted to know why the engagement party next weekend is an engagement party and not a wedding."

*Oh shit!* Derek wasn't the one dragging his feet. My last trip to LA left me with a lingering sliver of doubt I couldn't quite shake. Why was everyone in such a hurry?

"What did you tell them?"

"I told them they'd have to discuss it with my little planner, and if they found out any details to let me know. So, what's it going to be, Miss Kelly? I'd marry you tomorrow if that's what you wanted."

"I know, it's just that—"

"You need more time?"

"Yes."

He pulled me into his arms. "Of course. Take all the time you need, my angel."

I nestled against his chest. "Thank you."

His kissed the top of my head. "Well, if we aren't

getting married tomorrow what do you want to do? It's the weekend. We could go away for a few days, just the two of us. New York, Hawaii, Miami. Where would you like to go?"

"The mall."

"The mall?"

"Yeah, I just want to do something normal. Can we go to the mall?"

"Yes, of course. We'll go to the mall. Goodnight, my sweet girl, I love you."

* * * *

The next afternoon, Derek and I strolled hand in hand through The Galleria Mall. It was a bit of drive, but we couldn't go to The Fashion Show Mall on the Vegas strip. There were too many tourists and Derek would be hounded for autographs. Surprisingly, if we steered clear of the strip, we could go out unnoticed by his adoring fans.

Of course, I couldn't stop adoring him every second. Even in his casual shorts, T-shirt, and baseball hat, he was sexy as hell. I loved the way he kept his body in constant contact with mine. His simple, sweet touches sent a low rumble through me. It told me and anyone passing by the food court, I was his.

He nearly charmed my pants right off in one of the department store dressing rooms. His hot dog on a stick was irresistible. Obviously, it was time to head home before I succumbed and got arrested by a mall cop.

As we traveled toward the exit, Derek took note of the Christmas in July decorations and stopped. "I just thought of something. I get to spend my first Christmas with the girl of my dreams. We should pick something out, anything you want, sweetie."

He spoiled me sufficiently already. However, I couldn't deny him. I couldn't deny him anything.

I happily bopped over to the decorations perusing all the wondrous holiday items. Thoughts of Derek and I snuggling in front of a fireplace, sipping red wine, and making love, joyfully whirled my brain. In the past, my Christmas memories overflowed with sadness. Now I was here with my beautiful fiancé, realizing Christmas could be as magical as it was before my mom died. Our future together shined as bright as the decorations before me.

Derek looked like a kid himself examining the model train under one of the trees.

I threw my arms around his neck. "Did you have train like that growing up?"

"I did, but my older sister, Dina, never let me be the conductor."

"Well, you can drive my train anytime, Mr. Pierce."

He grinned in his devilish way. "Considering you have the sweetest caboose I will take you up on your offer, Miss Kelly."

Derek picked up the large box and handed it to the

salesperson. He encouraged me to continue my search for something special. When I moseyed back to the ornaments, I spotted it. I couldn't believe my eyes, it was an exact replica of a manger scene; identical to the one I had growing up when Mom was alive. I'd never seen another one like it before. I ran my fingertips over every figurine. Tears pricked my eyes. I sensed my parents' presence taking me back to those enchanting Christmas memories. I shut my eyes wishing they could've met Derek. Then it hit me, this manager scene was a sign. They granted us their blessing. I picked up the angel and clutched it to my chest.

Derek draped his arm around my shoulder. "Hey, this is beautiful. Is that what you want?"

Overcome with emotion I glanced up at him with tears in my eyes and nodded.

He wiped them away with his pad of his thumb. "Did you have a manger scene like this when you were little?"

"Yes."

"Come here, sweetie." His arms wrapped around me with his chin resting on my head. "Then we will get this manger scene and ten more if that's what you want. I'm going to see to it, all of our Christmases will be everything you ever dreamed of and more. I love you."

In that moment, it became crystal clear. I gasped. "I know when we should get married."

He beamed. "When?"

"On Christmas Eve, at your house in LA, in your

living room. It has the big mantle and fireplace with space for a Christmas tree on each side. We could get married standing in front of the manger scene. It would be like my parents are with us. Is that okay?"

"Yes, of course its okay, it's perfect. Christmas Eve. I can't wait."

His lips graced my mouth with the most exquisite kiss. "And now I need to get the future Mrs. Derek Pierce home. I'm making love to you the rest of the day. You are mine."

"I am yours."

"I'm never letting go."

* * * *

"Feel me, baby." Derek anchored us on the apex of our simmering climax. He enveloped me in his love, with his body weight pressing me into the mattress. Yes, I was his. I couldn't wait to be his wife. Today erased that tiny sliver of doubt. I was going to marry this man. This was so right. He treasured me with exotic, needy kisses and was about to bathe my walls with his cum.

"Are you ready? Are you ready to come with me, sweetie?"

With my eyes fixed on his, I panted, "Yes."

Our stunning release felt like slow rolling thunder fluttering through our bodies. Then it gripped us and flew us to the stratosphere. Derek crushed me to his chest, draining every last drop of our essence.

His large hands splayed on my back and calmed my post-orgasmic quivers.

When the ability to speak returned, he held my face. "Christmas Eve can't get here soon enough, my angel."

"I'm so excited. We have a plan."

Derek smiled. "Yes, the perfect plan for my perfect girl. I'm actually a little surprised you want to get married in LA. I know you don't like it there."

"I don't, but your living room in LA has the mantle and fireplace. Plus, I don't think you'll be bombarded with phone calls from your manager or publicist on Christmas Eve."

"That's true. Actually, I won't be bombarded with phone calls next weekend when we're there for the engagement party, so who knows, maybe LA will start to grow on you. Do you think it could?"

I didn't want to answer that question, luckily for me there was something else growing, Derek's cock. My mouth helped itself, tonguing him until his erection rose to its complete glory. Good save, now I couldn't answer the question. After all, it was impolite to talk with my mouth full.

# Chapter Fourteen

Valerie Bennett and Charles Pierce's sprawling estate was out of this world. It was positively Shakespearean. Our engagement party resembled *A Midsummer Night's Dream* plus modern day amenities and minus the guy with the donkey head. Although it was quite possible, there could be a jackass or two.

From the luxurious linens to the breathtaking flowers and beyond, this party was fit for a princess. When I was little girl and sang, "Someday My Prince Will Come," I didn't think he'd actually show up. But he did. He completely swept me away.

Maybe LA wasn't so bad. Since arriving, Derek remained my sweet, loving, attentive Vegas Derek. He also arranged for Steve, Scott, Julia, Phillip, Brooke, Tom, Aunt Mary Jane and Uncle Bill to fly here on his plane. They were also staying at his house. Unfortunately, the Peterson's, my chorus girls, and their hubbies were on a cruise together. Lacey and Shannon stayed behind in Vegas and held down the fort at the country club.

Punctual as ever, Derek and I showed up an hour early. He awaited his sister, Dina's, arrival in the house, while I soaked in the majestic sight of our party from the large, charming gazebo. In front of the gazebo, the pool magically turned into a dance floor. Band members began lugging their instruments to a raised platform directly across from me. There were two bars with staff for food and cocktails. Tables circled around the dance floor. Valerie arranged for a special family table inside the gazebo, which included my entourage.

I spotted Derek in the distance sporting his million-dollar smile. He looked so handsome in a dark suit with perfectly coiffed dark-blond hair. He strolled in my direction carrying a bouquet of white hydrangeas, fresh from one of his mom's flower bushes. I loved them. They were delicate with just the right amount of fragrance. Maybe I should include them in my wedding bouquet. Yes, my prince had come. All my dreams were coming true.

"Sweetie, you look beautiful." He adorned my lips with a kiss that was swoon worthy. The way his eyes took me in made me feel beautiful in my new white dress. It was simple, but elegant with a slight plunge in the front and a lower one dipping down the back.

"Thank you, you look beautiful too. Are those flowers for me?"

"Of course, and there's something else." He placed the white hydrangeas on the table. "I have a confession to make. I peeked at the dress you're wearing tonight. I wanted to make sure this went with it. He produced the most off the hook, crazy great, amaze balls necklace I'd ever seen. It was a platinum chain with a diamond that matched my engagement ring.

"Oh, my God, Derek, it's incredible. I love it. I mean, you totally shouldn't have, but it's stunning."

He fastened the necklace around my neck and playfully nibbled my shoulder.

"Hmm…I'm going to spend the rest of my life spoiling you, so get used to it, no arguments."

I teased, "No arguments? You have met me, right? I'm afraid I can't promise that."

"Young lady, you're lucky my parents and sister are headed this way or I'd take you over my knee and give you the spanking of your life."

*Well, fuck me.* His words triggered a pool of moisture between my legs. I was doomed. Now I would be in agony all night.

Delighting in my torment, he whispered in my ear, "You're wet, aren't you? Shall I rip your panties off?"

I exhaled, while my body flushed under his words.

Without skipping a beat, my devilish fiancé called to his family and they greeted us in the gazebo.

Derek's sister, Dina embraced me. "It's so nice to meet you, Nia. Finally someone in this family is my size."

Dina had Derek's striking blue eyes, but she was small framed, with brown hair flowing down her back, like me. She explained her two daughters and husband couldn't make the trip. Their summer schedule was packed with activities for the girls.

We still had thirty minutes before the guests descended on the estate. Charles popped open a bottle of champagne and proposed a toast to Derek and me. After one sip of bubbly, a phone's rude vibration interrupted our moment. It was Derek's phone.

"Sorry, I have to take this." He excused himself and kept the call short. When he returned, he asked his family, "Guys, could I have a moment alone with Nia?"

They all claimed they needed to do something and scattered. I braced myself, something wasn't right.

"I need to tell you something so you're not caught off guard. That was Aaron, and they've cast my new love interest for the next season of *First Bite*. He's bringing her to the party."

"Okay, that's fine, who is it?"

He sighed. "It's the last person I wanted them to cast, Mandy Hamilton."

Oh God. Mandy Hamilton was a former child star, turned teen queen, turned certifiable train wreck. She'd been in and out rehab so many times, she probably had a permanent room. Derek said *First Bite* would be her triumphant return to acting if she remained sober. The producers were sinking a fortune into this risky long shot. It was a risk they needed to take since ratings were at an all-time low. I didn't relish the idea of her coming to my engagement party. She was tabloid bait. It wouldn't surprise me if Mandy Hamilton had *TMZ* on speed dial.

The unwelcome news didn't damper my party mood when I saw my gang approaching the gazebo with Derek's family. Charles had a firm grip on Aunt

Mary Jane. She beamed in a gorgeous royal-blue dress. Valerie escorted Uncle Bill. He appeared a bit stiff and favored his left leg, but was handsome as ever in a navy suit. My friends looked so impressive they might be mistaken for celebrities. Julia glowed in yellow chiffon and Brooke dazzled in a sexy gold-toned dress. Phillip, Tom, Steve, and Scott were equally dashing in their finest. I was so thrilled to see them; I couldn't decide who to hug first.

I peered up at Derek. "I can't wait for you to meet Aunt Mary Jane. She'll take one look at you in that suit and faint."

She didn't disappoint. Aunt Mary Jane hugged Derek before she hugged me. She was tiny, but her enthusiasm nearly knocked Derek off his feet. "Oh, Derek, I've been dying to meet you ever since Nia showed me your bare butt on *First Bite*."

We all exploded in hysterics. Aunt Mary Jane was just warming-up. "Oh, my, you are so tall."

Derek glanced at me with a smirk. "Yeah, I get that a lot."

Mary Jane locked her arms around Derek's waist as if she was a human belt. "Bill, can you believe we're here, first the private plane and now this, if our friends in Wichita could see us now. I bet that old bag Ann Benson would be so jealous, she'd crap her pants."

More boisterous laughter ensued. Uncle Bill rescued Derek. "Good God, Mary Jane, you're going to squeeze the life out of the boy. You haven't even hugged our beautiful niece."

With that, warm embraces followed. Once we settled in with a cocktail, the guests arrived and the band played their first set. After a brief catch-up with Aunt Mary Jane and Uncle Bill, I chatted at length with Steve and Scott. Man, it was so good to see them. Steve's dad was hanging in there, not improving, not getting worse. They said they knew they did the right thing by moving home. Steve hired a nurse so they could come to our party, but would leave first thing in the morning.

The gazebo provided the perfect spot for people watching. Julia and Brooke were in heaven. Valerie and Charles's guests were a smorgasbord of fascination. There was old money, new money, and pretend money. Oddly enough, the people with the old money had the newest faces.

I preferred hanging with my peeps in the gazebo. In my opinion, it was the cool kids' table. While Derek, Valerie, and Charles mingled with their guests, Dina hung with us. Perhaps the LA scene wasn't for her either.

I was just about to send out a search party for my fiancé when Keith and Tim landed in the gazebo.

I popped out of my chair to greet them. "Hey, guys. You want to hang out with us?"

"Yes, please. I'm all mingled out," Tim said. "There's nothing more frustrating than trying to carry on a conversation at a party in LA. You feel like you're a place holder until someone famous catches their eye."

"Amen!" Keith added. "Nia, this gazebo is like a refuge camp for wayward minglers. Give us your poor, your tired, your, oh look, better people."

We all chuckled a bit and then I made the proper introductions. Except for the brace on his hand, Keith was as good as new. Thank God, there was no permanent damage from the car accident.

Surprisingly, the band played a Pitbull song. Aunt Mary Jane sprang from her seat. "I love this song. They play it in my Zumba class at the YMCA. Nia, we have to dance."

She dragged me out to the dance floor. Julia, Brooke, and Dina followed. Aunt Mary Jane stole the show. Wow, could she move. A crowd formed around us, and Aunt Mary Jane soaked up the attention. She was something else, what a corker.

The band did a one-eighty. They slowed things down and played, "Unforgettable." It was our song, our first dance. Before I could search the crowd for Derek, his arms snaked around my waist and he nuzzled my hair. "May I have this dance, Miss Kelly?"

I teased, "I can't, Mr. Pierce, it's against the rules."

"I'm afraid I'll have to insist."

He tipped my chin and blessed my mouth with a soft kiss. It was such a surreal moment. I was marrying the man of my dreams, actually the man of many women's dreams. He held me close while we swayed to our song, telling me how much he loved me.

I gazed up at him with wonder. He took my breath away.

"What is it, sweetie?"

"It's you, you being so incredible to me and my friends, oh, and let's not forget Uncle Bill and Aunt Mary Jane."

He laughed. "Trust me. I will never forget our Aunt Mary Jane."

"Oh, our Aunt Mary Jane? So she and Uncle Bill are already family?"

"Of course, Mom and Dad didn't have brothers and sisters. I grew up without Aunts and Uncles. I think I've been missing out."

"Now you know why I was so sad when they moved to Wichita."

"Trust me, I get it. You and she have a lot in common. You're both great dancers and quite the handful."

"But I'm your handful."

He pressed his lips to my forehead. "You're my everything."

Surrounded by hoards of party guests, I still felt safely tucked in our bubble. The song changed keys sailing into its final chorus. We were completely lost in one another, until Aaron tapped Derek on the shoulder.

Derek said in a cold tone, "Not now, Aaron, I'm dancing with my fiancée."

"Sorry, it's Mandy Hamilton. She's here and she isn't sober or patient. Give her five minutes and I'll get rid of her."

Derek shook his head. "Tell her she'll have to wait."

"Honey, I'm fine. Go talk to her if you have to. Do your thing. I've got my peeps in the gazebo."

"Actually, that's an excellent idea. My parents are in there talking to Tom and Phillip. They have much more experience dealing with drunken starlets."

Derek motioned for Aaron to head to the gazebo. Aaron steadied Mandy in her six-inch stilettos. We hung back as they made their way. Mandy stumbled and spilled some of her red wine. Her wineglass was the size of my head. What were the producers of *First Bite* thinking? Courtney Love would take one look at this girl and say, "Now that's trashy."

Like seasoned pros, Valerie and Charles welcomed Mandy pretending not to notice her intoxicated state.

When Derek and I approached, Valerie smiled, but had steam coming out of her ears. Mandy's inebriated presence had everyone on edge.

It was sad. She was once Hollywood royalty and she drank or snorted it all away.

*Oh, shit!* Snorted it was right. No wonder everyone looked outraged. Mandy had what I could only assume was a vial of cocaine in plain sight.

Aaron attempted a normal introduction. "Hey, Mandy…Mandy… Uh…as requested here's Derek your new costar. You remember him from the audition, right?"

This poor girl needed help, not a TV series. I remembered her from her teen queen days. Heck, I was a fan. Now she stood before me, skin and bones with dirty blonde hair. Her once bright eyes were glossy and bloodshot.

Her voice sounded like a tractor mowed over her vocal chords. "I auditioned? I'm Mandy Hamilton, I don't audition."

Derek regarded her cautiously. "It's good to see you again, Mandy. I look forward to working with you. This is my fiancée, Nia."

"It's nice to meet you, Mandy," I offered my hand, which was the stupidest thing I could've done, because she two-fisted it with red wine and cocaine.

She leaned in my direction and mumbled, "Yeah… whatever." Lost her balance and poured red wine all over my beautiful white dress.

I gasped and everyone flew in to action. Valerie said to Derek, "We'll take care of Nia. Mandy better be gone when we get back."

Charles added, "Aaron, remove her at once."

The next thing I knew I was in Dina's old room with Dina, Aunt Mary Jane, and Valerie. They peeled me out of my wine-soaked ruined dress.

"That's was awful. Are you okay?" Dina asked.

"I think I'm still in shock. Wouldn't you know it, the one time I don't wear black."

"Don't worry. I bought four extra dresses. You can wear one of those. We're practically the same size. We sisters have to stick together."

*A sister?* Dina would be my sister and was already stepping up to the plate. I should too. I should shake this off and go back to the party.

Aunt Mary Jane piped up, "Dina's right, you'll change and then we'll dance the night away. I haven't shown off all my moves yet."

We chuckled a little, and Valerie responded, "Ladies, would you mind if I had a moment with Nia?"

Aunt Mary Jane and Dina politely obliged.

On her way out the door Dina said, "The dresses are hanging on the back of the bathroom door. I think there's even a white one."

"No thanks, no more white dresses for me, ever."

Valerie retrieved the dresses. "I hope you don't mean that. Wedding dresses are usually white."

"I'm sorry. I was just kidding. Actually, we've set the date. We're getting married Christmas Eve."

Her face lit up. "Oh, Nia, that's wonderful. I was concerned after Lena put out that story about her and Derek and then Mandy. Well, let's just say, it would only be natural to have second thoughts."

"To be honest, it hasn't been easy. You were right when you said it takes a strong woman to be with a man in Hollywood. But I love your son. I want to marry him more than anything."

She embraced me. "That's all I needed to hear." She grabbed the strapless dress. "Red, I think. It says I am strong and confident. You should wear this."

I slipped off the robe I borrowed from Dina and tried it on. It clung to me in all the right places. Valerie was right. I felt like a superhero.

On our way back to the party, Valerie checked in with their head of the household, Bradford. He was entrusted with the donation envelopes for Sammy's Place. I'd let Mandy Hamilton throw ten glasses of red wine on me if meant helping more victims of domestic violence, and providing a safe haven for them, their children, and their pets. Bradford assured us the charity would be pleased.

Valerie and I went back to the gazebo and resumed the festivities. Derek spotted me and hightailed it in my direction. He wrapped me up in his arms, whispering in my ear, "I'm so sorry. I should've told Aaron not to bring her. I had no idea."

I wasn't going to dwell on Mandy a second longer. I peeked up at him. "It's okay. It's just a dress. Dina lent me this one. You like?"

I twirled as he drank me in. "Like it. I love it." He shouted to Dina, "Hey, sis, you're not getting this dress back."

She laughed and winked while everyone welcomed me back to the party. We ate, drank, and made merry. Then Aunt Mary Jane couldn't take it anymore and dragged all of us to the dance floor. Well, everyone but Uncle Bill, he said his knee was acting up. Charles kept him company.

The band, Big Daddy and the Wings, were quite

eclectic. They dabbled in every genre from the classics to hip-hop. We all had a blast, especially Aunt Mary Jane. Uncle Bill watched her and just shook his head. Yep, we had much in common, including being a bit too much.

As the evening ended, I forgot all about Mandy. Derek and I were attached at the hip. Most of Charles and Valerie's friends were long gone and replaced by the cast and crew of *First Bite*. With the exception of a couple of actors who took themselves too seriously, and Oliver Rock, I liked the *First Bite* bunch, especially Madison.

Big Daddy and the Wings announced they were taking their last break before the final set. Derek was the last man standing. All the other guys were inside watching the end of a Dodger game that was in extra innings. Dina, Valerie and Aunt Mary Jane were enthralled in conversation with Madison as they began their slow journey toward the house.

Brooke, Julia, Derek, and I left the dance floor together. The next few moments felt like slow motion. I heard a collective gasp leave our mouths. I couldn't believe my eyes. Talk about shock and awe, this was shock and appalled and disgusted. *What the fuck!* Oliver Rock and Lena Rozwell strolled into our engagement party as if we were long lost friends. I wanted to slap the smug expressions off their faces as they sidled up and invaded our space.

Oliver extended his hand. "Congratulations. Nia,

how lovely to see you again."

Derek took a protective stance in front of us, and refused to shake hands. "Oliver, what are you doing here?"

"You invited me, remember?"

Derek gritted his teeth. "Don't pull this shit with me. You know exactly what I'm talking about. You brought Lena to fuck with us. You've had your fun. Just go."

My blood boiled at the sight of them. They came to hurt us, to remind me the exotic, raven-haired beauty was naked in Derek's bed.

Lena opened her wretched mouth. "Aren't you going to let me congratulate the future Mrs. Derek Pierce?"

Derek turned to us seething. "Julia, will you and Brooke take Nia up to the house."

"I'm not going anywhere."

"Nia, listen to me. Go to the house, now."

Julia and Brooke motioned for me to go with them. I conceded.

Lena shouted after me, "How much is Derek paying you to keep his secret?"

I stopped. "What secret?"

"Clearly, the man is gay. You must have some kind of arrangement. I offer him myself in Paris and he turns me down for a dog like you."

"You bitch," I screamed and lunged for her.

Derek caught me around the waist and held me

back. "Nia, don't."

"Oh look, he can't control his dog."

With one swift move, Derek handed me off to Julia and Brooke and got in Lena's face. "You need to get the hell out of here before we call the police."

I broke free from Julia and Brooke. Derek put a hand out to stop me from charging. "Actually, you need to get the hell out of here before I smack the crap out of both of you. And for the record, Lena, Derek didn't reject you in Paris because he's gay. He rejected you because he didn't want to sleep with a filthy whore."

Lena leaped forward. Derek blocked her, and said to me in stern tone, "Go to the house with Julia and Brooke. Do it."

As they scurried me to the house, police sirens whirled in the distance. Tom and Phillip charged down the hill to Derek.

Tom said to us as they passed, "Valerie called the police. Everyone's inside. Don't let Nia out of your sight."

I pleaded with Julia and Brooke. "I should be with Derek."

"No, let the police deal with them. You'll only make it worse," Julia responded in her direct Julia way.

"I could've taken her."

Brooke tightened her grip on me. "If you did, you'd be giving her what she wants, another story to feed the press."

Maybe they were right. Damn it. I screwed up.

When we got inside, Valerie ushered us up the back stairs to Derek's old bedroom.

The three of us flopped on the bed is disbelief. Lena's cruel barb resonated in my head. I really wasn't good enough for Derek. The whole world thought so. I put my head in my hands and let out a huge sigh.

"Are you okay?" Brooke asked.

"I'm fine. I know it's stupid, but what Lena said got to me. Julia would call it a famous person problem, so I guess it doesn't count."

"Oh trust me, it counts. No offense, but you just had the worst engagement party in the history of engagement parties."

She was so right. My party sucked ass. I actually giggled a little. "It really was awful, the worse engagement party, ever."

We cracked up and rid ourselves of our uncomfortable shoes. Brooke and Julia exchanged a sheepish glance. Something was going on.

"Okay, out with it. You two know something I don't, so spill."

Julia confessed, "Well, there is something, but we didn't want to steal your thunder."

"Please, I'd pay you a million dollars, steal away."

"Brooke, you go first."

She showed me her left hand. "Tom and I are engaged."

Shrieks of glee erupted in the room. Brooke's ring was as gorgeous as the bright smile on her face. "He proposed yesterday, right on the tennis court."

I squeezed her tight. "I'm so happy for you, I could burst."

"If you don't release me from your death grip, I just might."

"Oh sorry. I'm a little excited."

"Julia, you're up."

Julia took my hands in hers. "Nia, I'm pregnant. I'm going to have a baby."

Sheer joy glowed in the room.

I embraced her with care. "Oh, my God. How far along are you?"

She squelched her tears. "Not very, I just found out today. I peed on the stick right before we left for the airport. Phillip said it was too soon to tell people, but the second I stepped on Derek's plane, I blabbed to everyone. I've been waiting for the right moment to tell you all night."

Steve and Scott appeared in the doorway with a bottle of champagne, glasses, and a bottle of water.

"So, this is where the party went," Scott said.

I motioned for them to come in. "Yeah, some party. I got red wine poured on me, the evil Lena shows up, and the cops were called."

Steve touted, "Now you know how *The Real Housewives of the OC* feel."

We all busted out laughing, while Scott handed the bottle of water to Julia and popped the champagne. I took the moment in. The original five TV binge watching gang holed up together in Derek's Pierce's childhood bedroom. Surely none of us imagined that when we watched him on the "Naked Season," sixty-nine times.

I sighed. "I wish you guys didn't have to go back to New York tomorrow morning."

"We wish we didn't either. We'll miss all the fireworks," Scott replied.

I hoped tomorrow would be drama free. The plan was to have a small gathering at Derek's house, although, once again I couldn't wait to leave LA.

"Hey," Derek said from the doorway. He looked spent. "Lena and Oliver are gone. The police escorted them off the property. Technically, Oliver was invited, but Lena could be charged with trespassing if Mom and Dad decide to press charges."

"Are they going to?" Julia asked.

"As long as Lena and Oliver don't go to the press about tonight, they aren't. That's the deal we made. It's the only way to keep Nia threatening them, out of the tabloids."

Everyone's eyes focused on me. Why did I get the blame? "Lena's the one who came uninvited."

Derek rubbed the back of his neck in frustration. "Guys, could you excuse us? There's a car waiting downstairs. We'll meet you back at my place."

I said good night to everyone and squeezed Steve and Scott extra tight since they were leaving right after breakfast.

Derek shut the door and walked over to the bed. I couldn't read him at all. Was he angry or upset our party was a giant bust?

"Are you mad at me?"

He removed his suit coat, slung it over the chair in the corner, and shoved his hands in his pockets. "I'm not mad, I'm disappointed."

He rolled up his sleeves and paced the floor. Visible tension encased his jaw. "I can't protect you if you don't do what I say. I told you to go to the house and you didn't listen."

"Lena started it. She called me a dog. And you know what, she's right. It's what everyone thinks. I'm not good enough for you."

He softened. "Nia, that's not true. Don't say that."

Crocodile tears dripped out of my eyes. "I'm sorry I disappointed you. I didn't mean to, but this is so hard. I feel like I'm constantly waiting for the other shoe to drop…and… I–I just want to go home."

"Baby, please don't cry." He cradled me in his arms, and rubbed my back. "Hey, I'm sorry too. I wanted to give you an engagement party you'd remember for the rest of your life."

"No chance in hell I'll ever forget it."

Derek cracked a slight smile and wiped away my tears. "There's my girl." He scooped me up onto his lap. "So, tomorrow I'm thinking, we might need to change our plan. And before you freak out, let me finish. What do you say we take everyone back to

Vegas with us? We'll pack up everybody on my plane and Mom and Dad's, and party at our house. Sweetie, I want to go home too."

My thoughtful, incredible fiancé got me. I perked right up. "Mr. Pierce, that is one fucking great plan."

"I'm so glad it meets the Nia Kelly planning seal of approval."

Derek caressed my face and touched his lips to mine.

I broke our kiss. "Listen, I need to tell you something. I know I screwed up tonight. I shouldn't have engaged with Lena. I'll try to do better, but keeping my mouth shut has never been my strong suit."

He grinned in that adorable way that sent my heart flying. "It's one of the many things I love about you, your mouth, your beautiful, dirty mouth."

Then he gave me that look. I parted my lips and granted him my beautiful, dirty mouth. His soul-stirring kiss was so intense. I couldn't tell where my breath ended and his began. He clutched the nape of my neck and poured all of his love into me. I disintegrated under his masterful prowess. I ached for him, all of him.

He released me and panted, "I need to get you to bed, my bed. I have to be inside of you."

I pleaded, "This is your bed too."

"No, not here, my sweet girl."

I unbuttoned his shirt. "There's a house full of people waiting for us. Even if they're all asleep, they'll hear us. Please, I dig your funky leopard Tarzan sheets."

It was then I took a gander around Derek's old bedroom. It was like a weird nineties time capsule.

"Nice try. But, no, we'll go back to the house, I'll put you to bed and we'll make love. And if the whole house hears us, who cares, or maybe you could practice keeping your mouth shut. Just give me a minute. I can't face my parents with this."

I glanced down and there was a giant tent issue in his pants. I giggled. "Okay. I love you."

He held me close. "I love you too."

I nuzzled against him. "Derek, I still hate LA."

"I know, baby. I'm starting to hate it too."

# Chapter Fifteen

"To Tom and Brooke on their engagement, may your score always be love serving love." Phillip raised a glass to the happy couple in our backyard.

Julia teased. "How long have you been waiting to say that little gem, Player?"

"Since the two of them met."

"Hey, Phillip, awesome toast," Tom said. "It was short and sweet, just like my Brooke." They kissed, and the air filled with a chorus of, "Ahs."

Now it was my turn to toast Julia and Phillip. "When Julia told me she was pregnant last night, I kept thinking this will be one lucky baby. Everyone says babies are a blessing, and they are. But this little one will be blessed with more love than she or he knows what to do with, so, to Julia and Phillip and little Nia or Noah, here's to the blessing of love."

"Damn pregnancy hormones," Julia said and dabbed her eyes.

More toasts and well-wishes followed. Derek's plan to fly everyone to Vegas was brilliant. After a teary goodbye to Steve and Scott, we packed up two planes for our short flight. Even Marcus, Derek's chef, made the journey. He told me to stay out of the kitchen while he prepared our feast. Somehow, Aunt Mary Jane charmed her way in so she could make her to die for Mac and Cheese, a secret family recipe.

After our delicious banquet of yummy, everyone settled in to relax, except for Derek and his parents. There was a bit of tension between them as they headed upstairs to Derek's office.

Julia and Brooke bonded with Dina in the pool, and the guys played with the dogs. Molly was quite the competitor. She outran Sammy almost every time they threw the ball. Coco looked like she said, "Screw it," and scampered to the shade.

For once, it wasn't blistering hot. The meteorologists said it was a cool down, which meant no humidity and a mere ninety-six degrees. Uncle Bill, Aunt Mary Jane and I stretched out on lounge chairs under the patio cover.

Jake approached and said, "Miss Kelly, I'm driving Marcus to the strip to meet his friends. They're staying at the Aria. He wanted me to tell you he'd catch a ride back to LA with them. I'm sorry to bother you with this, but Mr. Pierce appears to be in a meeting."

"Jake, it's no trouble at all. And please, call me Nia?"

Aunt Mary Jane turned and her mouth gaped open at the sight of Jake and his biker good looks. She popped out of her chair like a teenager. "Nia, who is this handsome devil?"

"Jake, this is my Aunt Mary Jane and Uncle Bill. Jake is Derek's driver and my..." I didn't finish the sentence. My Aunt and Uncle didn't know about Larry Wall or the recent drama with Nick's family and Melissa. The less they worried the better.

Lucky for me, Aunt Mary interrupted in her trademark human belt squeeze. "Well, if I need to go for a ride, I know who to call. I guess Nia doesn't know any ugly men. Do you have a girlfriend?"

Uncle Bill peered over his magazine. "For crying out loud, Mary Jane, let the boy do his job."

I said to Jake, "Sorry, she does this a lot."

Even rough around the edges Jake got a kick out of her. Once I pried my aunt off him, he left and we resumed our relaxed state.

Uncle Bill was so serene he snoozed and snored away. Aunt Mary Jane grasped my hand. "I'm glad we came to Vegas. To be honest I was a little concerned after last night. Now I see your life here is home."

She totally got it. She summed it up in one sentence. "I love it here. I always have. LA and I go together like oil and water."

"Or as your mom would say garlic on cheesecake."

It was crushing how much I missed my parents. Especially today, it was Mom's birthday. "Have you been thinking about her today as much as I have?"

"I think about her every day, but even more on her birthday. I miss her and my brother too. They had a once in a lifetime kind of love. That's what I see when I look at you and Derek. Now me and the snoring clodhopper do all right for the most part. But the way your dad loved your mom was something extra special. It's the way Derek loves you."

"Thank you for saying that. It's what I need to hear. Oh, I can't believe I forgot to tell you. Evelyn called me."

Aunt Mary jolted in her chair. "Well, now there's a fucking bitch for the ages."

I cracked up. "I could listen to you say the F-word all day."

"You and I can get away with it because we have innocent faces."

I raised my glass to hers. "Agreed."

"What did the legend in her own mind, Evelyn want?"

"She was trying to butter me up since I'm engaged to a celebrity. I called her on it and said a few choice words. I don't think I'll ever hear from her again."

"I wouldn't put anything past her. I know you're supposed to forgive and forget, but when it comes to that woman, I just can't do it. She's the reason your dad and I had a falling out."

"What exactly happened between you and dad? I remembered you came for Christmas when I was fifteen and then I didn't see you until I graduated from high school."

She swung her legs around to face me. "Well, I hadn't been inside your parents' house since your mom's funeral. I couldn't believe what Evelyn did to the place, all those fucking teddy bears and wicker. And there wasn't one picture of you or your mom in the whole house."

"I know. She got rid of all her things, even the Christmas decorations. She would've gotten rid of me too if she could've."

"I mentioned the pictures to your dad and he told me to keep my opinions to myself. Then I made things worse by telling him the truth. I said, the only woman you've ever really loved would be disgusted by the way you're allowing Evelyn to treat her child. He kicked me out and we didn't speak until you graduated from high school. After that, I only saw him a handful of times. Now he's gone. Your parents were taken way too soon."

I slid over to her chair and held her hand. "They were, but you and I have each other and the snoring clodhopper."

A noise escaped Uncle Bill that sounded like a worn-out chain saw mixed with a foghorn. She chuckled slightly. "I hope you know how much we love you."

I clasped both my hands around hers. "I do. I love you guys too. I also think Mom wouldn't want us to be sad today. She'd want us to celebrate. You know how she loved a good party. So, I'm going to find Derek and tell him we need to make the most of every moment."

I stood up. Aunt Mary Jane reached for me. "Nia, Brian and Angela would be so proud of you."

A lump formed in my throat when she said my

parents' names. I hadn't heard them in such a long time. I'd forgotten how well they went together, as if they were one syllable. Evelyn wouldn't allow the name Angela to be uttered under any circumstance. I almost expunged their names from my memory. I couldn't say one without the other. They belonged together, and now my parents, Brian and Angela Michaels were together.

I kissed her cheek. "Thank you."

"You go find Derek. I'm going to cool off in the pool. Better yet, maybe I'll accidentally on purpose fall in and Phillip and Tom can rescue me."

She giggled like a schoolgirl the entire way to the pool while I made a beeline for Derek.

When I reached the top of the stairs, I heard muffled raised voices coming from the office. It sounded like Derek and his dad clashed about something. What could they possibly argue about on a beautiful day like today? We should all be celebrating.

I debated knocking. Then I realized, this was my house too and opened the door. Three heads snapped in my direction in shock. I guess I should've knocked.

Charles sat behind the desk with a pained expression. Valerie was in the wing back chair and Derek's six-foot-four-inch frame verged forward in long strides stopping me at the door.

"What's going on?" I asked.

He swallowed hard and said sternly, "Nothing. Go back downstairs."

I peered around Derek. "Charles, what is it? Why

does everyone look upset?"

Derek was about to chastise me, but I pushed past him, and spotted a stack of legal documents on the desk.

"Will someone please tell me what's going on?"

Charles glanced at Derek and responded, "I'll tell you."

"Dad, don't."

"Derek, she's going to found out sooner or later. You can't keep it from her."

"Of course I can. She doesn't need to know because there isn't going to be one."

Charles threw his hands up in the air.

I pleaded my case to Valerie, "Valerie, please."

She sighed. "The two most stubborn men I know are fighting over your prenuptial agreement."

What a relief! The way they talked, I feared Derek had some secret baby mama who scored a guest spot on Maury Povich.

"Where is it? I'll sign it."

I picked up a pen off the desk and Derek ripped it out of my hands. "No, you're not signing anything."

Charles pounded his fist on the desk. "Derek, be reasonable. Nia, I assure you, this protects you too."

I shrugged. "I'm sure it does. I told Derek it's not a problem."

Derek grabbed my shoulders. "And I told you, no. That's final."

Charles begged, "Please, son."

"Dad, mind your own business."

"This is our business, when your mother and I pass, you and Dina will inherit a small fortune. I'm trying to protect that too."

"I don't need your money."

With Derek towering over me, I glared up at him. "Derek, stop. Listen to me, today is my mom, Angela's birthday. She would've been sixty. So there will be no more fighting. I'm signing the prenup."

Charles handed me the pen and pointed to the places requiring my signature.

Derek made one last attempt. "You're not even going to read it?"

"Nope, because I trust Charles. If he says it protects me then I'm good with that."

"I assure you, Nia, it's quite fair," Charles said. "I hope you understand this doesn't mean we aren't thrilled you two are getting married."

"I know that. And while we're on the subject of the wedding, Derek, you should understand I will not be saying the word, obey."

Valerie cracked a gleeful grin. I finished with a flourish. "In case you've forgotten, there's a party downstairs. The way I see it, you can stay up here and be mad, or you can come downstairs and have some fun. Life is short. Valerie, would care to join me?"

"Absolutely." We glided out of the office arm in arm. When the men were out of earshot she whispered, "Bravo, darling, that was excellent."

* * * *

The sun went down and we all tucked in to Marcus' divine leftovers. Everyone also raved about Aunt Mary Jane's Mac and Cheese. I thought if I plied her with enough wine she'd cough up the recipe, but she didn't.

Derek was finished sulking. In fact, he bound in the kitchen donning a sly smile.

"What's that look for, am I in trouble, again?"

"No, quite the opposite. Is everyone outside?"

"Yeah, I told them I'd clean up. Dina offered to help and Brooke said, don't even bother. I guess they know me too well."

"Good, because I have something for you, I meant to give you these last night, but I put them in the safe and then I forgot to bring them to LA."

He reached in his pocket and produced a fancy velvet box. When he revealed what was inside I nearly died, earrings to match the necklace I wore last night. The clear stones were the same size as the diamond on the necklace. *Father, Son and Holy crap!* They probably cost twice as much as the necklace. These over-the-top sparklers were remarkably exquisite. I was almost afraid to wear them. Then, I got over it.

I beamed. "Oh, my God! Derek, they're so beautiful. You really have to stop spoiling me. It's too much."

He gripped my hips and planted me firmly against him. "Remember, young lady, I spoil you and no arguments."

"But I don't need to be spoiled, I just need you."

He slid his hands under my bikini bottoms and shoved them to the floor. "That sounded like an argument."

His hands cupped my naked butt cheeks. I gasped. "Derek, someone could walk in…at…any… Oh, what the hell."

It wasn't as if my ass mooned the picture window. Derek pressed me against the island, with his erection grinding into me. What kind of delicious torment did he have in mind?

His lips found my neck, spurring on my arousal. I whispered, "I need you. I need you to fuck me. Can we go upstairs?"

His grip tightened. "No."

I panted. "Please."

He growled in my ear, "Another argument?"

*Oh shit!* This could be a little wicked payback for my performance in the office today.

"You should be prepared for a lifetime of them, Mr. Pierce. I don't know how to obey."

His eyes burned through me. "I'm going to teach you." One long finger glided down my crack and tucked inside my surprised pussy. I flinched and caught my breath. Surely, he wasn't going to take me in the kitchen with a backyard full of people. Neither one of us could see the door. My deviant desires nearly got the best of me, but eventually good judgment prevailed. "I can't see the door. We won't know if someone's coming."

Two fingers burrowed inside me. "Trust me, someone will be coming. You'll come for me, won't you?"

I tried to break his hold. "No, I can't see the door."

He released his grip, bent me over the island, and smacked my ass. "Can you see the fucking door now?"

I whimpered, "Yes."

"Do you want to argue about anything else?"

"No, I want to come for you."

"Good girl, now spread your legs. Let me inside my greedy pussy."

I opened my legs and invited him in. I heard Derek's shorts hit the floor. He pressed one hand on my back and the other firmly on my hip. The entire length of his shaft rammed me in one powerful thrust. I was such a slut for his cock. I clutched the granite counter top rejoicing in his violent blows. He was fucking me into a pile of ash, with his barbaric rhythms. My greedy pussy awarded him with a flowing stream of juices. He gained momentum and punished my cunt with rapid, rough fuck strokes. I released muffled cries and held on tight.

He grunted. "That's my baby. Take my cock."

He came all the way out, and crammed himself back inside me like a missile. My body was firmly shackled to the island as Derek's hands bore down on my back. His ruthless discipline of my saturated hole rushed me to the edge.

I was so close. He had me in such a salacious frenzy. I didn't care who walked in on us now. It could be Derek's parents, Aunt Mary Jane, or the entire cast of *Big Bang Theory*. I wanted to come for him.

Derek groaned and spanked my ass. "Come, come now."

I shattered around him, giving him everything.

"That's it. Good girl."

His forceful release broke free inside me, as his cock twitched and spewed. *Son of a bitch, I can't believe we did that*. That was one pussy pounding of a fuck.

Derek hummed in praise, while delivering sensual kisses on my back. "Thank you for not arguing with me, my sweet girl. You're fantastic."

He almost had to pry me off the kitchen island with a spatula. I turned to face him with spongy legs, and he gathered me up in his arms. Then we realized there was a male and female dripping 'jizz' situation. Derek got a paper towel and tended to me. We put our bottoms back on and grabbed more paper towels to tidy up the island and floor.

Without warning Aunt Mary Jane appeared in the kitchen. "Are you kids still cleaning? We've all been wondering what's taking so long."

I stuttered, "Well…uh…w–we were finished and

then I–I spilled something and then Derek really spilled…and…I–I guess we made a mess."

She wasn't buying what we were selling. "Well, in that case, I'll let you get to your cleaning." She sauntered off. "Oh, to be young again."

Derek cracked up. "She didn't believe us."

"Nope, not for a second. I hope she doesn't tell anybody. If word gets out no one will want to eat dinner at our house ever again."

The bell rang. I invited Lacey and Shannon to come by after work. We went to the door together in our disheveled just-fucked state to find Shannon and Walter. Crap, she brought Walter.

Concealing my disappointment, I greeted them warmly. I also asked about Lacey. Shannon pointed to the curb. Lacey and Jake were chatting. I actually heard Jake laugh aloud. Good for them.

Shannon spotted my earrings. "Nia, those are gorgeous. Are they an engagement present?"

Derek replied, "They're more like I'm sorry I forgot them in the safe and didn't give them to you last night present."

I chimed in, "But he did give me the matching necklace, it's gorgeous too."

Shannon said, "I can't wait to hear about your party."

"I'm afraid I'm not drunk enough yet to tell you about that. We're going to run upstairs real fast, everyone is in the back. We'll be out in a minute."

"Okay, girl, I know the way." Shannon and Walter trucked outside.

Derek and I hurried upstairs. When we landed in the bedroom he said, "I think we should put your earrings back in the safe."

"At the risk of arguing with you, can I leave them on so I can show the girls?"

"Of course, but if you want to get in the water give them to me, deal?"

I extended my hand, teasing. "Deal. I wouldn't dare disobey you."

He grabbed my hand and yanked me into his arms. "I don't believe that for a second, Miss Kelly. You're a very bad girl. I look forward to a lifetime of disciplining your bottom." His hands went right to my ass. "In fact, there is long list of offenses, starting with the prenuptial agreement. Before you try to defend that little stunt you pulled, I have one thing to say about it." He caressed my face and gazed at me in pure love. "I'm sorry your parents aren't here to celebrate our engagement and your mom's birthday."

"You're not mad?"

"No, my angel, I'm not mad. I understand now. Of all the things I want to give you, more than anything, I wish I could give them back to you."

I flung my arms around his neck and pulled his lips to mine. "My parents would've loved you as much as I do."

"I would've loved them too, so much."

* * * *

We resumed our party. All the girls went nuts for my earrings. At one point Phillip said, "Derek, you're making the rest of us chumps look bad."

Aunt Mary Jane and Uncle Bill said goodnight and trotted off to bed. Everyone else fell out in assorted stages of exhaustion in lounge chairs around the pool. Even the pooches were tuckered out. I plopped myself down between Julia and Brooke.

"You totally owe me and Brooke," Julia touted. "We kept your Aunt Mary Jane out of the kitchen for as long as we could so you and Derek didn't get caught."

"Get caught doing what?"

"You know exactly what she's talking about," Brooke replied. "I've seen you clean your kitchen a hundred times. You're like the Energizer Bunny. It takes ten minutes at the most."

Julia piggybacked onto their theory. "Yeah, so after fifteen minutes Aunt Mary Jane says she's going to go help you and we saved your ass. Were we right?

I confessed, "Yes!"

The girls squealed and Julia added, "You and Derek are the two biggest nymphos in the world."

"You're one to talk. You're knocked up. Speaking of which, do you want us to cancel our Napa trip at the end of August? It won't be any fun for you if you can't drink wine."

"No, I don't. Phillip and I talked about it and we realized once the baby comes we won't get a chance to travel as much. So, we are in. I wish Brooke and Tom could come."

"I wish we could too, but Tom's going on tour for a month. I told Lacey, Shannon, and the other girls we'd have wine tasting at my place."

I asked joking, "Wine tasting or wine chugging?"

"We'll sniff, we'll swirl, and chug."

We giggled and took note of Shannon and Walter frolicking in the pool. What a flirt fest! They definitely appeared to be a full-on couple.

Shannon shouted to me, "Hey, Nia, can you take our picture? My phone is next to my purse."

I snapped a couple of cozy photos and put her phone back down. Walter and Shannon needled me to get in the water.

Derek was on the opposite end of the pool chatting with Dina. He heard the teasing. "Sweetie, if you want to get in the water take off your earrings. I'll put them back in the safe."

"I don't want to get in. I'm kind of tired."

Walter amped up the trash talk. "Tired? Oh, come on. I'll race you."

Shannon made a sour face. I politely declined his challenge. Walter backed off and asked me if I could get him a towel. I went to the edge of the pool with towel in hand. Walter grabbed me instead of the towel and I catapulted into the deep end. Stunned, I sucked in an enormous gulp of water. The dogs bark and Julia screamed. Two strong arms rescued me to the surface. Derek sat me down on a lounge chair and Brooke wrapped me up in a towel. Sammy snarled and barked at Walter. Molly raced to my side just like everyone else.

Derek's hands went to my face. "Look at me, baby. Are you okay? You're shaking."

"I'm okay, it just scared me."

Walter threw his hands up. "What's with this dog? You all act like I committed a crime." Phillip corralled Sammy.

Derek got in Walter's face. "That wasn't cool. She said she didn't want to get in the water."

"Man, I was just trying to have a little fun. It is a party."

"She just learned how to swim, so again, not cool."

"Okay, I get it, my bad. Nia, I'm really sorry."

The look of embarrassment on Shannon and Walter's face made me sympathize with them.

"No need to apologize. I'm fine. I should've been a good hostess and joined you guys, but I'm just a little tired."

Valerie intervened, "I think we're all a little tired. Perhaps we should call it a night."

Charles added, "Yes, we should. Valerie and I are flying back to Chicago with Dina early in the morning."

Before leaving together, Walter and Shannon exchanged awkward good nights and everyone else hugged me extra tight and called it a night.

Derek, Molly, and I stayed outside snuggled up together on the lounge chair gazing at the stars.

I pointed to the sky. "Hey look, you can see my star. See the bright, golden one. It's called the Almach. It's the first star of heavens great."

He kissed my forehead. "It's beautiful. I didn't know you had a star."

"Well, I guess it's everybody's, but it's my favorite. After my mom died, I'd look out the window and search for my star. It made me feel less alone, like Mom was looking down on me. Now when I see it, I think of Mom and Dad. Sometimes I talk to them."

Derek smoothed my hair. "If they could talk back, what do you think they'd say?"

"I think they'd say the same thing Aunt Mary Jane told me earlier today. She said they'd be proud of me and that I found someone that loves me the way Dad loved Mom. You know, my mom had dad wrapped around her finger."

"Well, that does sound awfully familiar. I hope they know how much I love you. I know we hit a rough patch. But I'm not going to allow anything or anyone to come between us again. What we have together is a once in a lifetime love. I'm never letting go."

Derek graced my lips with a soft kiss. Yes, just like Aunt Mary Jane said, a once in a lifetime love. I prayed to my star he never let go.

# Chapter Sixteen

We rose early the next morning to see everyone off. Jake drove Valerie, Charles, and Dina first, and then came back and picked up Aunt Mary Jane and Uncle Bill. I told everyone at breakfast about our Christmas Eve wedding plans. Dina regretfully informed us she couldn't come. Craig, her husband, already committed them to fly to Wisconsin to spend Christmas with his family. Aunt Mary Jane pulled me aside before they left and told me they might not be able to come to the wedding either. Her plan was to talk Uncle Bill into a knee replacement before the end of the year, even though Uncle Bill didn't think he needed one. My small guest list for the wedding shrunk in half.

After everyone left, I told Derek what Aunt Mary Jane said and he asked, "Do you want to change the date? I'll fly everyone back here next weekend. Just say the word."

I took a page out of Aunt Mary Jane's book, became a human belt around Derek's waist and peered up at him. "You are awfully anxious to marry me, Mr. Pierce. If I didn't know better I'd think you're trying to tie the knot right away so you can knock me up like Julia."

"Is that what you think?"

"*I do!*"

He played with my hair. "Of course, I want to have babies with you, but I think we have plenty of time for that."

"Well, someone isn't getting any younger, Grand Pa."

He fisted and tugged on my hair. "Well, someone must want a spanking, Nia."

How did he do that? He could turn me on just saying the word. I had to get to work, but I longed to slide my shorts down and bend over the loveseat in our bedroom.

His eyes danced in devilish delight. "I know you're wet. Turn around. You're going to be punished."

I faced the loveseat. "But I have to go."

"Are you arguing with me?"

"No, but I'll be late."

"First of all, I'm driving you to work, and secondly this won't take long. Be a good girl, and bend over the loveseat."

How could it not take long? Usually crazy, primal fucking followed a good spank. But I didn't argue. I was wet and desperate to come. I bent myself over the loveseat.

Torturing me further, Derek took his time sliding off my shorts and panties, and tossing them to the side. My ass burned in anticipation, it also had to get to work. What was he waiting for? "Fuck, Derek, I'm going crazy, and I'm going to be late."

His hand fondled my cheeks. "Someone has been a very bad girl this morning." He dipped a quick finger inside, pulled it out and perched it at my lips. "Look how wet. Suck."

I took his finger in my mouth and licked off my devious, fresh juices. All four fingers found their way inside and I slurped and sucked until they dripped in a thick sheen of my saliva.

Derek's wet hand cracked my ass. It stung and landed on my sex. The second spank caused a rush of liquid to dribble down my legs. "Four more spankings, Nia, and then I'm taking you to work." Four more quick slaps brought me to the sizzling edge. I was ready to hump the loveseat.

He caressed my pink bottom. "All done. See, I told you it wouldn't take long. Put your shorts on. I'll take you to work. But just your shorts, no panties, they're soaking wet."

I snapped my head up. "Please, I'm in agony. I'm so close."

He spread me open with his fingers, examining my soaked pussy. "Yes, you are. And you look delicious, but someone has to go to work."

His hand cracked across my butt one more time. He stood me up and handed me my shorts.

"You're really going to leave me like this?"

"Yes, I believe I am. And tonight when you get home, I'll make you scream like never before. I plan on eating and fucking my pussy until it's sore."

* * * *

I squirmed in the car seat. "You suck."

Derek laughed and squeezed my thigh. "Is my girl still in agony?"

"Yes. I can't believe you're sending me off to work without getting me off. I should've smuggled Buzz into my purse."

"It'll be worth the wait, I promise. What time should I pick you up?"

"The last thing on my schedule is a private spin class at four, so five o'clock. You know I can drive myself. I don't need you or Jake to chauffeur me everywhere."

"I'm afraid you do. I'm not taking any chances with your safety, especially after what happened with Melissa. I also bought the house next door so Jake can be close by. He's going to stay there when I'm in Vegas, and when I'm out of town he's going to stay with you at the house."

"I can stay by myself."

"Nia, there will be no argument when it comes to protecting you."

"Fine. I know when you say my name you mean business."

"What are you talking about?"

"Usually you call me sweetie, baby, or angel. Lately when you call me Nia, I know I'm in trouble or you mean business."

"Well, in that case, Nia, I can't wait until tonight."

"You better tell Jake what we're up to. If you make me scream he might charge with guns blazing."

"I gave him the rest of the day off. So, you are all mine, Nia, all mine."

He pulled up to the door. I unbuckled my seat belt, leaned over and kissed his cheek. "All yours."

* * * *

The day wore on at a sluggish pace. I found my normal multitasking self-distracted by thoughts of Derek. He kept me on my toes in the bedroom, varying between slow and gentle lovemaking and dominant, rough fucks. I loved it all. I never felt so free and uninhibited. My body was wired and in tune with him, his voice, his touch, everything, even my phone. No wonder I couldn't concentrate.

His text messages made me hornier. "I can't wait to taste you tonight and make you come again and again, Nia." I had half a mind to run to the bathroom and rub one out.

Shannon's knock on the door jolted me out of my naughty notions. "Hey, I just want to apologize again for last night. I don't know what got into Walter."

"I've completely forgotten about it. By the way, you two looked pretty cozy."

She floated into a chair, with a gleam in her eye.

"Last night was our first official date. We'd already made plans to hang out when I got the text about your party. He finally kissed me. He's a really good kisser."

"Really?" *Didn't they kiss the day of the deposition?* "You're lucky Brooke is the managing director. Things used to be super strict around here. We weren't allowed to socialize with the members. We weren't supposed to have sex with them either. I guess I broke a few rules when I met Derek."

"Oh speaking of Brooke, she popped in to show us her engagement ring. It's gorgeous. Yours is too. If I didn't love you two so much, I'd be so jealous I'd have to kill you."

"Well, you never know. Maybe Walter's the one."

"I don't know about that. I'd settle for a second date. He's coming in for a private spin with you. Maybe he'll ask me to do something after work."

"Maybe he'll ask you to do this." I pantomimed a make out session. "Oh, Walter, you're a good kisser."

As if on cue, Walter appeared in the doorway and caught me. Shannon and I howled in laughter.

Walter was less amused. "Did I miss something?"

Shannon scurried out of the room. I was left holding the bag of embarrassment. I swiftly changed the subject. "You're here early? The fitness room is free if you want to get started?"

"You read my mind. I have a last-minute appointment to show Steve and Scott's house. The client seems really interested, I hated to say no or cancel on you."

"Steve and Scott will be thrilled to hear that. Give me five minutes and I'll be right in."

"Thanks, Nia."

He left and I shot a quick text to Derek. "Getting off thirty minutes early."

He wrote back. "You'll be getting off numerous times… Nia."

I couldn't wait.

The class with Walter went swimmingly, despite him throwing me in the pool last night.

"You're the best, Nia. I know I say that all the time, but I've been taking spin classes over fifteen years and no one comes close to you. You're just so into it and entertaining. Next time, I'll bring a snack. It'll be like dinner and a show."

An actual laugh transpired between us. Who knew Walter had a sense of humor.

"That's funny. And thank you, I do try to entertain when I teach. It's really a bit of a trick so you don't notice I'm kicking your butt."

"You're like an adorable magician."

Did he just call me adorable? *Yikes!* I opened the door, crossed to the equipment closet, and carried on as if I didn't hear the adorable comment.

Walter placed his hand on my shoulder. "Hey, I'm really sorry about last night. Would it be too inappropriate for me to tell you, you looked so sexy in your bikini, I lost my head?"

"Yes." Derek's voice boomed from the doorway. He stalked into the room. "It's completely inappropriate for you to say that to my fiancée." He pinned Walter with a steely stare. "It's also inappropriate for you to touch her, got it."

Walter conceded. "I got it, sorry. I was just leaving. I'll see you tomorrow, Nia." He slunk out of the room.

Still reeling Derek fixed his stare on me. "You need to get someone else to teach his private classes."

I shut the door for privacy. "I can't do that and I won't do that. You're being ridiculous. It was no big deal."

"I know what I saw. He wants you."

"Well, he can't have me. And…wait a minute… Oh, my God…you're jealous."

"I am not. Now you're being ridiculous."

Finally the tables were turned. This was awesome. "You're like the mayor of jealous town. I mean, I've seen bossy Derek, even possessive Derek, but never jealous. I thought you were way too confident for that. Derek Pierce is jealous."

"Are you finished? If not, I'll need my two-drink minimum for this little show you're putting on."

"Oh come on, just admit it. I get jealous sometimes. How couldn't I? Half the world whacks off to you. And I know that for a fact because I did it all the time. During the 'Naked Season' I nearly wore out Buzz."

He shook his head and smirked. "Okay, I was

jealous. I don't like the way he looks at you. I never have." He snaked his arms around my waist and pulled me close. "Plus, when you teach you become even more irresistible. Half of your students whack off to you. And I know that for a fact because I did it all the time. When we first met I nearly wore out my palm."

We chuckled, and then he drew me in for quick peck. "Come on, let's get you home. I have a beautiful pussy to fuck."

"Yeah, you do, hundred percent."

* * * *

Derek gritted his teeth. "I'm not finished fucking you yet, Nia. I need you to hear you scream again. I want you to squirt your cum on my cock."

I wailed, "Yes, I'm coming. I'm coming, ah God!"

"Just keep coming, Nia. You're going to be fucked until you're sore."

A little jealousy went a long way with Derek. How were he and his penis still erect? He took me in the shower against the wall. Then he bent me over the loveseat and finished what he started this morning. The way he spread me open and feasted on my sex from behind hurled me to *kingdom-cuming!* Derek packed his cock into my quivering tight hole, and endowed me with a series of hearty thrusts. When his vigilant fingers found my billowy clit, it set off an avalanche of cunt spray. The room echoed with sounds of slapping wet flesh and my throaty cries of ecstasy.

Now my ragged body was on the bed with my legs on Derek's shoulders. He stood at the foot of the bed hammering every little pearl out of my nearly shattered pussy. The sight of his perfectly chiseled physique and his thick cock disappearing inside me forged a fresh set of orgasms. I didn't know if I could take another overwhelming release.

Derek quieted his strokes as his gaze washed over me. "God, you take me breath away." He placed my legs on the floor and eased out.

My body instantly craved him back inside. "Derek...don't."

"Sweetie, I'm not stopping." He picked me up and lay me in the middle of the bed. His eyes captured mine. "I want to take you nice and slow. I have to make love to this gorgeous body. I have to make love to you. I love you."

I opened every part of myself to him. "I love you too."

He climbed on top of me, taking me slow, like calm waves in the ocean. Our bodies hummed together in perfect harmony. Every part of his being cried out in love for me. His tender kisses, his soulful touches, and his crystal blue eyes said it all. I was home. I belonged. I was his.

* * * *

"You are a man of your word, Mr. Pierce. You fucked your pussy until it is sore."

We relaxed in the tub with a glass of wine, my back to his front. Molly was on the bath mat with a new squeaky toy. The warm water and Derek's arms soothed my worn-out flesh.

"That was one epic fuck, my girl. I hope I didn't hurt you. You would tell me if I was too rough, wouldn't you?"

I peeked up at him. "Yes, but it was perfect, like you."

He graced my lips with a soft kiss. "I think you've got that backward. You're the perfect one, the way you've always given yourself to me. The trust you've placed in my hands to bring you to new heights and never go too far. It's a rare gift. I treasure it."

Derek's sweet revelation astounded me. It was true. I entrusted him with all of me. It felt so natural from the start I never questioned it. Yet, I spent my entire life clinging to control every aspect. I used to despise surprises or the dreaded changes in life. After Mom died, change was synonymous with a new horrid reality. With Derek, it was different. After all, the night we met was due to a last-minute change of plans. He opened up a brand new world to me. Slowly I was able to release the burdens weighing me down. His love did that.

After our bath, Derek put me to bed. Before turning out the light, he rubbed lavender lotion on my back and bottom. Molly curled up at the foot of the bed. I nestled in my usual spot on Derek's chest. He turned out the light and said, "Goodnight, my sweet girl, I love you." My little family drifted off to sleep.

* * * *

The next day at work, I did a mental high-five to last-minute changes. Walter canceled his private spin with me. Talk about a pleasant surprise, the awkward meter should be dialed down by tomorrow.

Late in the afternoon, I was at the sports desk with Shannon. She lamented about Walter not asking her out last night.

"I am so sick of men. He's like the king of mixed signals. First, he kisses me and then yesterday, nothing. He didn't even say goodbye when he left last night."

"Have you heard from him at all?"

"Yeah, he sent me flirty text messages all night. I mean, which is it?"

"Maybe something happened. He did cancel. You could send a friendly 'hey, heard you had to cancel, are you okay' text."

"That's a great idea, thanks."

I picked up my phone, and checked the time. "Oh, I just remembered I need to send Derek a text so he and Jake can pick me up a little early since Walter canceled. I actually could leave now, if I had my car. This sucks."

"Yeah, it really sucks to be you. Two gorgeous

men are coming to pick you up and you're complaining."

"Good point," I responded and unlocked my phone to text Derek. Before I could send the message, Brooke rushed up to the sports desk.

"Nia, I need to talk to you, it's important."

We hurried in my office and shut the door. "Brooke you're scaring me. What's wrong?"

"It's Sonya. I just got off the phone with Sonya Reed. She wants to talk to you."

I was dumbfounded. The woman who helped Larry Wall and Nick try to kill me wanted to talk to me.

I thought my head would pop off. "What the fuck! This is crazy."

"I know. I almost hung up on her, but she said she could help."

"Help? Help with what?"

"I'm sorry, I don't really know. At first she spoke freely, like we were old friends, but then she didn't make much sense. Her sentences were fragmented. I'm still trying to piece it together. She said, 'I can help that friend.' She talked about her job at a food court and then she said, 'Your friend will need my help.' It was hard to hear her over the noise in the background. Here, she gave me her number."

I ripped up her number and tossed it in the trash. "There's not a chance in hell I'm ever speaking to her again."

"I think you're doing the right thing. Just be sure

you tell Derek and Jake. I'll double check with security and make sure the new hires know she can't set foot on the property."

"I wish I didn't have to tell them. After everything I put Derek through with Nick's family, I hated to add to his stress. I really felt like we turned a corner last night. I don't want to go back."

"Don't keep this from him. It isn't fair."

"But think about it, one of them drives me around like I'm freaking Miss Daisy. I can't go anywhere by myself, and Sonya can't come here. Maybe I don't have to say anything."

"You're going to tell him. It's the right thing to do. Julia would think so too."

"Oh, you went there. You threw the Julia card. You only get one of those a year."

"Is that because the rest of the year she's always right?"

"Yep, pretty much. Man, my therapist can't get back from maternity leave soon enough."

I'd been missing our weekly session. Derek and I had a two-hour appointment with Dr. Roma the day after tomorrow. Between the mess in LA and Nick's family we should've booked her for an entire week. Now, Sonya reared her ugly head and threatened the new peace we found. I should tell Derek and Jake, but not tonight. I'd been looking forward to another romantic whirlwind evening with my fiancé.

A quick rap on the door got our attention. It was

Derek, ready to take me home. I swiftly gathered up my things and scooted out before Brooke had a chance to say anything about Sonya.

When we settled in the car, I melted into him and drank in his scent. I couldn't wait to get home and crawl into our bubble. There was no way I'd let Sonya ruin it.

His kissed the top of my head. "Did you have a good day? I missed you."

"I missed you too, especially when I thought about last night."

"Are you still sore?"

I shrugged with a smile. "I'm not sore, but very mindful of where you've been."

He held me a little tighter. "Does that mean I've been on your mind all day?

"Only in the dirtiest way."

"That's my girl. I can't wait to get you home. I have a surprise for you."

"Really? I love surprises. I mean most surprises. Your surprises are the bomb."

Consumed with guilt, I realized I should tell Derek about the Sonya bomb. Then his finger tipped my chin and he graced my lips with the sweetest kiss. I couldn't do it.

* * * *

He blindfolded me with the bachelorette gift,

courtesy of Nancy. Molly followed us upstairs to the bedroom.

Derek untied the blindfold and said softly, "Surprise, baby. This is for you."

I couldn't believe my eyes. It was a beautiful jewelry armoire identical to my mother's jewelry box. The cherry wood, the silver handles, it was the same.

My mouth gaped open. "Oh, my God, Derek, how did you do this?"

"Do you like it?"

I nodded with tears rolling down my cheeks. "I love it, thank you. Thank you so much. This is the best present I've ever gotten."

Molly yawned as if to say, "What about me?"

We laughed and sank to the floor.

I cuddled on his lap and Molly piled on. Referring to the jewelry box I asked, "Where did you find it?"

"I may have had some help from someone special. I told your Aunt Mary Jane what I wanted to do and she pointed me in the right direction. And there's something else."

Molly and I moved and Derek went to the jewelry box. He retrieved a tiny, worn felt box and got down on one knee. "I know I've already asked you this question, but with a ring this special, I think I should do it again. Will you make me the happiest man in the world and be my wife. Nia, will you marry me?"

My body shook with emotion. Derek proposed to me with my mother's wedding ring. "Oh, Derek, I didn't think I'd ever see that ring again." Those were the only words I uttered before tears descended. Derek clutched me to his chest, cloaking me in his love.

When I was all cried out, he whispered, "Sweetie, you didn't answer the question."

"What question?"

"Nia, will you marry me? You'll notice I said Nia because I mean business."

I wiped my damp eyes on Derek's T-shirt and peered up at him. "Yes, I will marry you, Derek Pierce. I love you. I didn't think I could love you any more than I did yesterday, but I do. I love you even more."

"That's all I needed to hear." Derek captured the nape of my neck drawing me to his lips. We breathed as one, and our magnetic connection soared. Both of his hands splayed on my back crushing me to him.

His mouth blazed a trail down my neck igniting the heat. "I love you, Nia. I have to have you."

I whipped my top off. My breasts beckoned him to have a taste. My right nipple elongated under his suckling skill.

He gave me that look. "I don't pay nearly enough attention to these lovelies."

He gingerly scooped me up and laid me on the bed. Derek took his tear-soaked T-shirt off and climbed on top of me.

Then the doorbell rang. *Damn it!* Loud barking ensued as we retrieved our clothes.

"Are you expecting one of the girls?" Derek asked.

"No, plus they would've sent me a text."

We scampered downstairs together and opened the door. It was Shannon.

"Hey, what are you doing here? Is something wrong at the club?"

She produced my phone. "No, you left your phone at the sports desk."

"Oh, thank you, come on in," I said, and shot Derek a glance to see if he was mad.

The three of us trekked to the kitchen for a glass of wine.

She asked, "Was everything okay with Brooke? She seemed so upset when she asked to talk to you."

Again, I spied Derek to gauge his reaction. He was silent. I blew it off and changed the subject. "Do you want to come upstairs and see what the best fiancé in the world got me today?"

Shannon and I hurried upstairs, while Molly and Derek went out for a play.

When she saw my jewelry armoire, she gasped. "Oh, Nia, it's beautiful."

"And look, it's my mother's wedding ring. Derek proposed to me again."

Shannon's eyes filled with tears.

"Hey, what's wrong?"

"Nothing, I'm being stupid. Sometimes I feel like everyone else has found love but me. You're engaged. Brooke's engaged. Julia's pregnant. Lacey has Jake. I can't even get a second date. I'm really lonely."

"I'm sorry. I didn't mean to shove my big armoire of happiness in your face. I just thought you'd want to see it because you liked my earrings and now they have a house."

"I thought the earrings went in the safe?"

I examined the armoire. "Maybe not, it looks like it locks. Gee, I hope Derek will give me the key. After leaving my phone behind he might not."

"Don't be silly. I've never seen a man so in love with a woman before. I can't imagine him being mad at you for a second."

"You might be surprised."

"I texted Walter like you suggested. He said he canceled because he had a friend in town. When I drove by his house, the lights were on and there were two cars parked in the driveway. It's probably a friend with benefits."

My heart went out to Shannon. She was too good for him. I was at a loss for words. If you're honest and say, "You could do better than that steaming pile of dog shit," the next thing you know she'll be dating that steaming pile of dog shit, and I'd be the giant asshole. For once, I kept my mouth shut. I almost imploded.

Molly jumped on the bed and cajoled her. Derek brought us our wine, and remained quiet. Before long, Shannon took off. Derek and I were alone together in the bedroom. I couldn't take the silence anymore.

I picked up my phone to charge it. "Are you mad I forgot my phone?"

He sat on the bed with his back leaning against the headboard. "No, sweetie, I was bummed we got interrupted. Now, strip and get over here. I have two lovelies to attend to."

His words alone made my nipples pebble. "Whatever you say, no arguments."

I straddled Derek on the bed. He rolled my left nipple delicately between two fingers. A moan escaped my mouth. His other hand cupped my bottom, while his tongue swirled over both breasts. My moans grew to groans.

He whispered, "I want to make you come, just by doing this."

I exhaled, "Yes."

He granted me a firm pinch, which tingled and warmed my gooey center. Then, that happened. Rambunctious Molly surprised us and jumped up on the bed for a threesome.

I squealed, "Molly, stop. Oh, my God, Derek, she's licking my butt."

We were dying with laughter. Molly must've thought we were playing a game and my ass was the prize. The three of us resembled some of sort of naked slapstick routine. Molly tripped me up and I landed face down on the bed. Her puppy nose pressed into my butthole. I flinched and screamed. Derek distracted her with a squeaky toy. He threw it down the hallway and shut the door. I was cracking up in hysterics.

Between laughs I said, "She put her nose in my

bunghole."

Derek chuckled. "I guess she knows a good thing when she sees it. I've been dying to get in there myself."

I rolled on my back and Derek snuggled next to me. Butt sex was back on the table for discussion. I'd been thinking about it and growing more curious.

I mumbled, "I think maybe I want to try it, you know, someday."

He smiled in his sweet way. "Only when you're sure you're ready. I want it to be great for both of us. I'm willing to wait as long as it takes." He drew me close and grazed his fingertips along my jawline and across my lips. "Meanwhile, there are so many ways we can explore each other."

I grinned. "I'd let you motorboat me, but my boobs are so small you're liable to chip a tooth."

He cracked up. "With our luck tonight, if we tried to have sex right now we'd get interrupted again. Captain and Tennille will show up on our lawn singing, 'Muskrat Love.'"

"Who are they? Did they sing on a boat?"

"No, young lady, they were a husband and wife singing team. They had a song called 'Muskrat Love' and 'Love Will Keep Us Together.' My mom liked them. She played their album a lot when I was a kid."

"You mean back in the olden days when there were these mythical, vinyl, round things called records."

He hooked me around the waist. My naked body

was flush on top of his. He cracked my bottom with a quick slap. I yelped.

"Careful, Miss Kelly, you are dangerously close to going over my knee."

My stomach muscles clenched and moisture from my pussy dripped on Derek. He gripped my ass. "I can already feel how wet you are for me. I love it."

He didn't take me over his knee. But he did take me. In one seamless move, he sat up, got on his knees and slid inside me. Our trembling limbs clung to each other as we drove one another to climax. It was always passionate, always phenomenal, always together, always and forever.

* * * *

When we cuddled up in bed I asked, "Hey, I almost forgot. How did you get my mom's engagement ring? I'd always imagined my stepmother pawned it or something."

"Aunt Mary Jane gave it to me. I guess your dad thought the same thing. She told me your dad gave it to her when he married your stepmom. He wanted your future husband to propose with it. So, I did."

"That is so sweet of my dad, my Aunt, and sweet of you too."

His lips brushed my temple. "I'm sorry. I meant to tell you that earlier. I was caught up in the moment. I forgot."

"That's okay. We all forget things, like cell phones. I promise I'll try to do better. I know I make you crazy with the phone."

He cracked a slight smile. "Thank you. Actually, that reminds me. What did Brooke want to talk to you about? Shannon said you left your phone at the sports desk when Brooke came to talk to you. It sounded serious."

It was the moment of truth. Do I upset the apple cart and tell Derek about Sonya, or do I take a risk and not tell him? After the magical evening we experienced I didn't want Derek stressed-out again. I said it was work related. If nothing transpired from Sonya's phone call to Brooke, I could save Derek the worry, and he would never know about my little fib. After all, I lived in Vegas. I took a gamble.

# Chapter Seventeen

"Walter is here for his seven o'clock," Shannon said in a lighthearted tone.

I waved her into my office. "You seem awful chipper. Did he ask you out?"

"No, but I think he might. Late last night he sent me flirty text messages again."

"Did you flirt back?"

"A lady never tells. I'll let Walter know you'll be right in. Oh, and don't forget your phone."

I thanked her for the reminder, threw the phone in my purse and left it on my desk. I would grab it after class when Jake came to drive me home. I picked up my gym bag, locked my office and hurried to the fitness room.

Walter warmed up on his bike, only this time he pulled a bike out of the equipment closet for me too. I took it as a silent apology for what happened after his last class.

"Hey, thanks for setting me up. Do you have any special music requests?"

"I like the Usher song, 'Scream.'"

Of course you do, because all forty-something white dudes loved Usher. *What an odd request?* I played the song and he was really into it. For the first time I listened to the words, and holy shit, they were filthy. It talked about sex and making the woman scream and going all night long. Why did he pick that song? The uncomfortable meter in the room dialed way up.

After class, I fumbled about and made idle chitchat while I put the bikes and mats away. I wished Walter would leave, but he stayed even after the task was complete. A brilliant plan struck me.

"So, what are you and Shannon doing tonight?" I asked.

"Shannon? I wasn't aware we were dating."

"Oh I know, but you two looked so cute together in the pool. If you're not dating her, you should be. She's a great girl."

He cocked his head and smiled. "There are many great girls at the Mountain Heights Country Club."

*Oh, crap!* I continued my Shannon campaign. "You won't find another girl as wonderful as Shannon. She's the total package."

He stared at me intently. "I hope Derek knows how lucky he is."

*What the what?* Jake broke the awkward silence. "Miss Kelly, are you ready to go?"

*Hell yes I was ready!* I picked up my gym bag and ran to the car. Once inside I took a deep breath. Does Walter have a thing for me? The first time I met him he was so aloof. It made zero sense. Shannon was closer to his age, available, and interested. Plus, she was amazing. My head swirled. Do I dare tell Derek about Walter? Guilt already consumed me for not telling about Sonya's phone call to Brooke. I couldn't do this. I had to come clean and tell Derek everything. The Lena Rozwell situation spun out of control because Derek kept it from me. I wasn't going to go there. It was wrong.

I realized Jake wasn't taking me home. "Jake, where are we going?"

"Mr. Pierce is in a meeting. It should be over in about twenty minutes. He told me I should drive you there, and we would wait for him."

Geez, somebody should've told me. "Can you take me home? Julia's coming over, I have to take a shower and feed Molly. I'll only be alone for a half hour, it'll be fine."

"I'm afraid I can't do that. Mr. Pierce's instructions were implicit."

"I forgot to tell him Julia was coming over to plan Brooke's bridal shower. I'm sure he would let you take me home if he knew. I promise I'll text him right after I feed Molly, and tell him I changed the plan. Please? I'm dying to get out of these sweaty clothes."

Jake reluctantly drove me home. I fed Molly, took a quick shower and threw on some shorts. Then I remembered I promised Jake I'd text Derek. I raced downstairs to grab my phone. *Damn it!* I'd left my purse locked in my office. I was so screwed. All of my options sucked. If I didn't text Derek, tell him I changed the plan, and waited for him to come home he'd be mad. If I drove myself to the club, retrieved my phone and he found out I went alone, he'd be mad as hell. I weighed the odds. His meetings usually ran late. I could drive to the club, grab my phone, and arrive home before him. It was another gamble. I rolled the dice.

* * * *

I parked my Honda so close to the entrance of the sports club, I was practically inside the glass double doors. The place was empty as the sun disappeared behind the mountains. I unlocked the front door, hightailed it to my office, and snatched up my purse. My phone vibrated angrily. Crap, I was probably busted. I fumbled through my purse on the way out the door. When I turned I nearly fainted. Sonya stood in front of my car. In a flash, I jumped back inside and locked the door.

She put her hands up as if she surrendered. "Nia, I'm sorry, I mean you no harm. I need to talk to you."

With phone in hand, I shouted through the door, "No, you don't. Leave me alone, or I'll call the police. You'll end up in jail where you belong."

"Please, I want to help you."

Through the glass, I peered at the woman who hated me for no reason. She wore her same football helmet hair, but her body appeared frail under her worn, baggy clothes.

A trace of sympathy almost made me drop my guard, but I couldn't take any chances. My phone vibrated off the hook. I hit the ignore button and dialed 911. I held it up and showed her the screen. "If you don't leave right now I'm calling the police. I don't want your help."

She vanished quick as a cat. I slumped down on the floor, quaking with my phone clutched in my hand. I checked my text messages. There was one from Julia saying she was too tired to get together tonight, and the rest from Derek. It was a diatribe of outrage.

"Why aren't you home?"

"Where the hell are you?"

It got worse from there. *Fuck! Fuck! Fuck!* I was too afraid to open the door and run to my car. Maybe I should call Derek.

A rattle on the glass door scared the shit out of me. I looked up from the floor. It was Walter.

He said through the glass, "Hey, am I glad someone is still here. I left my wallet in my locker."

I was actually relieved to see him. I opened the door, let him in, and locked it behind us.

He asked, "Are you all right? What were you doing on the floor?"

"Um… I dropped my phone."

"Oh, I'll just run into the locker room and get my wallet."

I paced the floor. My phone was quiet, which made

me more anxious. Derek probably gave up on me and called the police, or sent out a search party.

When Walter returned wallet in hand, I asked, "Walter, would you mind walking me to my car?"

"You mean the car that's parked in the lobby?"

"Oh, you're right, never mind."

"Hey." He caressed my elbow. "Nia, are you sure you're okay?"

"I'm fine. Did you see anyone when you drove up here tonight?"

"No, it's like a ghost town. Practically everyone's on vacation." He released my elbow and placed his hands on my shoulders. "Why don't you let me drive you home?"

"No, that's silly, I'll be fine."

"It's no trouble. I came in my golf cart. I can drive you and walk home. I only live a few houses away."

My angry phone vibrated and insisted to be answered. "I have to go." We hurried out the door and I locked it behind me. Walter waited until I drove off before walking to his golf cart. My heart raced the entire way home. Derek would be beyond worried and pissed. I royally screwed up and it was time to face the music.

* * * *

I peeked inside the door as if I was dipping a toe in the ocean. Exactly how icy and rocky were the waves?

I sounded cool as a cucumber, "Hey sorry, did you try to call? I left my purse at work and…"

Derek rushed to my side and held me. "Sweetie, thank God, you didn't answer your phone. Don't ever do that to us again, Jake and I have been worried sick."

I spotted Jake in the kitchen. His face was ashen. I put him in a terrible position. I went to him and apologized.

Derek said, "Jake, you can go now. I appreciate you staying until she got home safe."

"Jake can totally stay. You're probably hungry. I'll make you a grilled cheese. You'll love it."

"Nia," Derek warned. "Jake isn't staying. We need to have a little talk about you taking off alone, right, Nia?"

Crap, he just doubled down on my name and he doesn't even know the half of it.

Derek saw Jake to the door and came back in the kitchen.

"Honey, are you hungry? I could make you a grilled cheese or I have some leftover pasta salad. It's the kind you like with tomatoes, red pepper, and mushroom."

He responded in a flat tone, "No, I'm not hungry. Nia, we need to have a talk. Come." He ushered me to the TV room. I sat on the sofa and he sat on the coffee table across from me.

His quiet demeanor threw me. I thought he'd be furious, but he stared calmly into my eyes and waited for me to speak.

I babbled, "I'm really sorry. I know you're mad and you should be. I blew it. I forgot my phone and I left alone to get it, which I'm not supposed to do for safety reasons. I shouldn't put myself in jeopardy and I should answer my phone." Thoughts of Sonya flooded my brain. It caused me to tremble with emotion. "And you're right about everything and I'm sorry, I'm so sorry."

"Hey, sweetie, are you shaking? Oh God, are you afraid of me? Come here."

He cradled me on his lap. "I'm not angry with you. I was just worried."

"I'm not afraid of you, but something happened."

He rubbed my back. "What happened? Please, talk to me. You can tell me anything."

I murmured, "I saw Sonya."

Derek's eyes grew wide. "What? Where did you see her?"

I scooted off his lap. It was downhill from here. "I saw her at the country club when I went to get my phone."

"Did she hurt you?"

"No, she was standing by my car. She said she was sorry and needed to talk to me. She said she wanted to help me. I held up my phone and dialed 911 and she took off."

"Why didn't you call me? It wasn't safe for you to go to your car alone."

"I–I didn't. Walter walked me to my car."

Jealous Derek bubbled up, "Really, Walter fucking James, how convenient."

"Derek, it wasn't like that. He left his wallet in his locker. If he hadn't shown up, I would've called you. But I also would've been alone until you got there. I know you don't like him, but I'm glad he was there."

He paced. "I'd like to know how Sonya got on the property. I thought they were supposed to tighten the security. Tomorrow we're filing a restraining order against Sonya and talking to Brooke about this. Something has to be done. I'll hire extra security myself if that's what it takes to keep you safe."

"Sonya could have old friends that work here or maybe she's friends with members at the club. But it still doesn't make any sense because Brooke told me yesterday she was going to talk to security about not letting Sonya through the gate."

"What did you say?" *Oh, fuck!* Now I really blew it. This isn't how I intended to tell him. I could see the light bulb going off in his head and the steam coming out of his ears. "What exactly did Brooke tell you yesterday?"

I hung my head in shame. "She told me yesterday Sonya called her because she wanted to talk to me. I was going to tell you, I swear."

"Is that the 'work issue' I specifically asked you about? Nia, did you lie to me?"

I rubbed my hands on my face and willed myself to

disappear. My gamble crapped out before my eyes.

Derek raised his voice. "Nia, answer me, did you lie to me last night?"

I mumbled, "I didn't mean to. I'm sorry."

"You are un-fucking-believable!"

He pounded the wall. I'd never seen him so angry. I cowered on the couch. He flattened his hands on the wall and steadied himself. He exhaled and lumbered to the kitchen in silence. I watched him from the couch grab a beer and gulp it down. Our eyes met and his disappointment and frustration bore down on me.

I whimpered, "I really was going to tell you about Sonya."

He stayed in the kitchen. With a quiet, hardened tone he replied, "I can't protect you, if you don't listen to me. And I sure as hell can't protect you if you lie to me. What's it going to take, Nia?"

Derek marched out of the kitchen. I stared at the floor, drowning in a muddy pool of my own making. I should've told him. I fucked-up. I fucked-up big time.

Molly toddled in and jumped on the couch. At least she wasn't mad at me. We hung out in the TV room, but Derek never came back downstairs to talk. He probably locked himself in his office.

It was after eleven when Molly and I climbed the stairs. Derek wasn't in our bedroom. He wasn't in his office either. He was in the guest bedroom at the end of the hallway. He couldn't be any further away than if he slept in the car.

For now, maybe it was better to leave him alone. Molly and I tucked in bed watching TV. My eyelids grew heavy during a rerun of *Rules of Engagement*. Obviously, I had no clue what they were.

* * * *

"Hello? Is anyone there?" I called down a long, dark hallway lined with gold doors. They enticed me and lured me inside. The room was pitch-black. The floor felt sticky. I was stuck and rendered immobile. "Derek! Derek, help me." An uneasy stillness filled the darkness. I bent down to untie my shoes, so I could escape. My hands instantly bolted to the floor. I heard Sonya's voice. "They are coming for you. They will find you." One by one, they rose out of the floor, cursing and screaming at me—Larry Wall, Nick, his parents, and Melissa. They swiped me with their claw-like hands. I was a lamb led to slaughter. I screamed at the top of my lungs, but I couldn't hear myself. "Derek, Derek, where are you? Please help me! Derek! Derek!"

"Nia, wake up." Derek shook me. My eyes popped open and I let out a blood-curdling scream.

He grabbed my shoulders. "Hey, it was just a dream."

My eyes focused and filled with tears. "Please forgive me. Please, I'm sorry. Can you forgive me?"

He wiped away my tears. "Of course I forgive you. Please don't cry. Do you want me to hold you?"

I nodded and Derek pulled back the covers. I took my usual spot on his chest. I snuggled. "Thank you."

His lips brushed my forehead. "For what?"

"For holding me and forgiving me. I hate it when we fight."

"I hate it too."

"Are you still very angry with me?"

"Yes, but I don't want to be."

"Would it help if I explained why I didn't tell you last night?"

He sighed. "I don't think so. Just close your eyes for me and go to sleep. If you have another bad dream, I'll be right here."

I laced my fingers in his. "But I just want to say…"

Derek's voice grew weary. "Nia, please don't argue with me. We have two hours with Dr. Roma tomorrow. We'll talk about it then. Go to sleep."

I didn't say another word. This whole "keeping my mouth shut" thing blows. Maybe Dr. Roma had a pill for that.

# Chapter Eighteen

"Derek, you look like you want to say something else. I have time if you'd like to keep going." Dr. Roma's calm voice resonated in the room.

We hashed out every detail since Lena Rozwell planted her story. It was like an emotional spring-cleaning. I told her about Sonya. How I kept quiet about her phone call to Brooke. I took full responsibility for it and said my intention was to save Derek the stress.

Derek said tentatively, "I do have something else to say. I need your help, Dr. Roma. I need to know what to do when I get angry with Nia. With her history of abuse I try hard not to raise my voice, but sometimes I'm so frustrated, and the idea that I have to be so careful creates more frustration. Does that make any sense?"

"Yes, it makes perfect sense. We all have a temper and constantly suppressing it under the enormous strain you've both been under isn't healthy. Nia, do you express your anger freely?"

"Lately, I express every emotion freely whether I want to or not. It's one thing I don't have any control over."

She smiled. "I'm not suggesting you scream and shout at each other, but you need to release your anger in a healthy way. Derek, if you get upset with Nia, I recommend you give yourself a timeout, go for a run, call a friend to vent, something like that. Nia, you need to give him space. Normally nothing gets resolved in the heat of the moment."

"He has given himself a timeout, but it feels more like a shut out." I replied. "He ends up sleeping in another room. I don't like it."

"I think it's important to aim for more balance in your relationship. Instead of not sleeping in the same room, set a time limit for Derek's space, something you're both comfortable with. Nia, I also think your ultimatum about never going to LA is a little extreme. In addition, Nia never being left alone is too confining. Give each other some breathing room and see how that works."

Derek piped up, "I'm going to have to disagree with you about Nia being alone. We have a security issue at the club and it's just not safe. She was alone for fifteen minutes last night and look what happened with Sonya."

"Derek, I think Dr. Roma's right. One of the reasons I didn't tell you about Sonya's phone call to Brooke was because I knew I would never have another moment to myself. I'll consider LA if I could drive myself to work once in a while or be at home without Jake being around."

Tension gripped his face. "I'll think about it. I don't want to smother you. I only want to keep you safe."

Dr. Roma said, "Our time is almost up. There's just one more thing I'd like to address. We've discussed Nia's control issues at length and you're making great strides. It's important to recognize your need to control little things like food and everything being in its place is because when you were young so many big issues were out of your control. It seems you're letting go of the things you can't control and focusing on the ones you can, but flexibility or being more spontaneous would also be good for you. Derek, you're the complete opposite. You're very easy going and don't feel the need to make a plan and stick to it, but with everything that's happened you are trying to control things you can't."

I jerked up straight in my seat. "Did you just say he was a control freak?"

Dr. Roma stifled a grin. "We don't like to use the word freak, Nia. I just want Derek to be aware part of his frustration could stem from not being able to maintain control of everything, like what happened with Sonya, or Lena and Oliver showing up at your party."

Derek jumped in. "I wouldn't say I have control issues."

My outside voice blurted, "I would."

He shook his head. "What I would say is when I try to keep a situation from spinning out of control and I ask Nia to do something, which is in her best interest and she doesn't do it, it drives me crazy...and...it hurts."

"How does it make you feel to hear that, Nia?"

In that moment when I glimpsed Derek, it finally sunk in and took hold. "It makes me feel awful. Derek, I'm sorry."

He reached for my hand. I met him halfway. It was what we needed to do for our relationship, meet halfway.

"I think that's a good place to stop for the day. You both should be proud of yourselves. You're doing great work."

* * * *

"Jake, I have a meeting with Martin, so I'd like you to take us home. I'll drive myself to the meeting and you stay with Nia."

Derek climbed into the car next to me. The last thing I wanted to do was argue, but did he not hear anything Dr. Roma said?

"Don't you think I could stay by myself for a little while? It's been such a long day. I just want to soak in the tub, alone."

I'd been up since six a.m. We took Molly for a quick jog. Then drove to the police station and filed a restraining order against Sonya. Next, we went to security. Brooke combed through every second of tape from last night while Derek bawled out the guards, again. Unfortunately, there wasn't a single scrap of suspicion. Did Sonya scale the fence or hide in someone's trunk? It baffled us. I worked for a few hours in my office and then we endured our lengthy session with Dr. Roma. I needed to decompress.

Derek pondered my request. "Sure, if that's what my girl wants. See, I'm not such a control freak after all."

I giggled. "Well, I don't know about that. Welcome to the club, Mr. Pierce."

"You're really getting a kick out of this, aren't you?"

"Dr. Roma might be my new best friend."

"Come here." Derek took my mouth in a sizzling kiss. I evaporated under his relentless tongue and soaked him in.

When he released me, I heaved. "Wow, what was that for?"

He glided his finger along my jawline. "It was for my beautiful fiancée, and a little coming attraction. We have some making up to do. I want you to relax in the tub and think about me fucking you, but don't touch yourself. I want all your pleasure."

What was this man doing to me? With just a few words, I squirmed in my seat. "Or you could go to that meeting, never. How does never work for you?"

Derek smiled. "I'd cancel it if I could. I can't wait to be inside you."

In order to take my mind off my burning need I asked, "Can you tell me about it? You and Martin have been meeting a lot lately."

"What I can tell you is I'm working on something. Something I've wanted for a very long time. Martin knows all the players in Vegas. That's all I can say for now, but trust me, if it works out you will be one happy lady."

"I wish you could tell me more, but I won't argue. See, I'm learning already. I'm letting go and trusting this is in my best interest."

"That's, my good girl. I think Dr. Roma was right about finding balance."

"I think she was too. I'm going to be more spontaneous if it kills me."

* * * *

I kissed Derek goodbye and hopped out of the car. I promised to turn the alarm on and double-check all the locks. After feeding Molly, I soaked in the tub and did exactly what Derek said. I thought about him fucking me. I resisted the urge to dip a finger inside myself because I got an idea, a fantastic, spontaneous, *fuck-rageous* idea.

I told him I'd whip up something delicious for dinner. I decided it should be me. I ran downstairs naked and cleared the chairs away from the dining room table. I spread a beach towel and myself as the centerpiece on top of the table. My phone beeped five minutes ago. It was probably Derek texting that he on his way home. When he walked through the door, he would find me on my stomach as the main course. The anticipation fired a wicked yearning through me. This was it, my moment of spontaneity realized. He turned off the alarm. Footsteps approached.

Naked on the table I said, "Dinner is served, Mr. Pierce." *Holy fuck me!* It was Jake! I screamed and rolled off the table. "Oh my God, I thought you were Derek. Don't come any closer, I'm naked." Damn it, my left wrist broke my fall and it throbbed. I groaned in pain.

Jake stammered, "I–I'm sorry, Miss Kelly. I–I swear I didn't see a thing. Are you okay?"

I whimpered, "No."

"Okay, let me help you. I'm not looking. I'm going to throw you the towel."

I covered myself, and Jake bent down to help me. *Why, God, why?* Spontaneity could kiss my bruised butt.

Jake's steely, gruff demeanor appeared shaken. "Where does it hurt?"

I showed him my swollen left wrist and he hurried to the kitchen for some ice.

"Miss Kelly, this doesn't look good. Mr. Pierce would want me to take you to Quick Care."

I couldn't go back there. When I moved here, I made an appointment with Julia's gynecologist, but had to wait eight weeks. I went to the nearby Quick Care for a follow-up visit after my miscarriage and fall down the stairs.

"I think it'll be fine. What are you doing here anyway?"

"Mr. Pierce's meeting was running long. He wanted me to stay with you. Martin is driving him home. He said he sent you a text."

"I didn't get it because I was lying on the table. I'm so sorry and mortified. I can't imagine what you must think of me."

"Miss Kelly, I didn't see anything."

"You're a horrible liar, and you might as well call me Nia. We are way past being formal."

A slight grin split his face and reached his sparkling green eyes. If Lacey was hitting that, she was one lucky girl. He examined my wrist more closely and I winced.

"You really need to get that checked out."

"Fine, there's just one problem. I don't think I can dress myself."

"I'll call Mr. Pierce and tell him what happened. Once he finds out you're injured, he will want Martin to rush him home. Can you get up?"

"Um…I think so. Could you turn around?"

Jake spun on a dime. "Yes, forgive me."

I hoisted myself upright and hobbled upstairs to wait for Derek.

* * * *

"Sweetie, what happened?"

I was lying on our bed covered in the beach towel. My nurse, Molly, couldn't get close enough.

"I fell and hurt my wrist." I removed my ice pack and showed Derek.

"How did you fall?"

"Jake didn't tell you?" Derek shook his head and I flushed with embarrassment. I sighed. "Well, I was trying to be spontaneous. I wanted to surprise you. I was lying on my stomach on the dining room table. I was naked, you know, like 'Nia, it's what's for dinner.' I heard my phone beep and assumed it was you saying you were on your way home. I didn't read it because I was already on the table. Jake walked in and shocked the crap out of me. I rolled right off the table."

"You know what they say when you assume."

"I definitely made an ass out of myself. I flew off the table and my wrist broke my fall." My left shoulder, hip and knee ached too. Unfortunately, I bruised like a banana in the summertime.

The notion of Jake seeing me naked sunk in. "Did Jake see you?"

"I don't know how he could've missed it. I sprawled out for the world to see. It was meant for your eyes only."

He pressed his lips to my forehead. "Do I need to speak to him about this?"

"Oh God, please don't. I think he was more embarrassed than I was."

"Okay, let me take a look at your wrist, can you

wiggle your fingers for me?"

I wiggled them easily. I hoped it meant no Quick Care. "Good girl, just to be on the safe side we should get it checked out. You could have a small fracture." I opened my mouth to argue and he stopped me. "Nia, I insist. Let me help you get dressed."

*Crap!* He said my name and I insist. I sucked it up and we drove to the nearby Quick Care.

They pulled my chart, took me back for an X-ray and put us in a room.

My Doctor looked like Doogie Howser. Were there no grownups available?

Doogie asked, "Exactly how did you fall?"

"Well, it was…just an accident. I'm really clumsy."

"Could you be more specific, Miss Kelly?"

There was no way I could. If I endured any more embarrassment today, I'd implode like a cherry bomb. "Like I said, it was just an accident. Is it broken?"

"There's a slight hairline fracture. It should heal quickly. Mr. Pierce, would you mind giving me and Miss Kelly a moment alone?"

Something odd was going on. Derek said, "Yes, I would mind. My fiancée didn't want to come here in the first place. I'm not leaving her side."

"I don't want Derek to leave. If you have something to say you can say it to both of us."

Doogie studied my chart again. "I'm sorry to be so blunt, but your evasive answers about your injury and your chart leave me no choice. Miss Kelly, did you injure your wrist or did Mr. Pierce?"

"Oh no, you have it all wrong. Derek wasn't even home when I did this. What does my chart say?"

"It says the trauma to your eye and your miscarriage was domestic violence. I have to know how you hurt your wrist."

Cue the cherry bomb! "I was waiting for Derek, naked on the dining room table, only Derek didn't walk through the door, our driver Jake did. I screamed and rolled off the table. If you don't believe me, go ask our driver Jake. He's the red-faced gentleman outside in the black car."

Doogie's eyes popped out of his head. I swear I gave him his first grey hairs. Now there was a blushing man in a lab coat. "Forgive me. I was just doing my job. I believe you."

Derek said, "No problem. We understand."

Doogie sighed. "What a relief. I love your show, *First Bite*. Season three was my favorite."

*Ah, the 'Naked Season!'* I chimed in, "Yeah, Derek gets that a lot."

* * * *

It wasn't until I tried to go to the bathroom that I realized being without the use of my left hand complicated things, especially since I was left-handed. How was I supposed to lift up my sundress and pull down my thong with only one hand? I stood at the toilet and called for Derek.

"What is it, sweetie? Do you have to go to the bathroom?"

My bladder was about to burst, but there was no way I could pee in front of him.

I nodded. "Can you help me off with my sundress?" He gently grasped the hem and pulled it off. "Thank you, I'm good now."

He didn't leave. "Baby, you're left-handed, how can you manage? You can pee in front of me. It's no big deal, let me help you." I clung to the sink with my right hand and he removed my thong.

My embarrassment level reached its max. "I think I've suffered enough humiliation for one day. I would rather teach a naked spin class than pee in front of you."

He smiled. "If you teach naked spin it better just be you and me. I'll be right outside the door if you need me."

I performed all my nightly rituals by myself and crawled into bed with my wrist wrapped.

Before Derek climbed in bed, he asked, "Do you want me to sleep in one of the guest rooms. I don't want to bump your wrist."

"No, I thought we were going to have make-up sex."

"Didn't you hear the doctor? He said no vigorous activity for at least a week. You need to heal."

"Well, I wasn't going to do it with my wrist?"

He chuckled. "I'll make you a deal. If you go to sleep for me right now, I'll lick your pussy first thing in the morning."

"Deal!"

"Goodnight, my sweet girl, I love you."

# Chapter Nineteen

"Jake saw Nia naked!" Lacey let the cat of the bag, or in this case, my bare butt. The girls at Brooke's bridal shower howled with laughter and demanded to know the entire story, which I divulged and slightly exaggerated for comedic effect. My story killed.

My wrist healed in just under a week. Plus, there was a silver lining. I couldn't teach spin, so I palmed Walter off on Christa, the new spin instructor, permanently. It was an excellent opportunity to escape Walter's unwanted flirtations. I had an inkling he would ask to switch back to me next week, but with our Napa trip around the corner, I could gracefully decline his request.

All the girls gathered at my house to toast Brooke, just as they did for me in June, only this time no blow-up penises and butt plugs allowed. Brooke wasn't a prude, but she was the most conservative of my friends.

Julia and I chose a theme of hearts and flowers. I filled the house with assorted bouquets of white hydrangeas. After seeing Derek's mom's hydrangeas, they quickly became my favorite flower. They were fragile, and didn't last long, but I loved them.

We all chipped in and signed Brooke up for a yearlong, weekly flower delivery from Marshall Morris

Florist. I'd never met Marshall, but the rest of my gals always used him. They said he was the best. Brooke was ecstatic.

She also delighted in her other gifts. Each one of us gave her a bottle of her favorite bubbly and something with hearts. I bought her heart decorated champagne flutes. Julia gave her a gorgeous vase with a heart etched into it.

The girls were very creative. Shannon got her a heart-shaped photo album, Nancy found candles, and Sharon bought her monogrammed dessert plates, with hearts, of course.

While I scoured the Internet searching for the champagne flutes, I found a black, heart-shaped cheese plate. I just couldn't say no and didn't. I purchased four of them and filled them with cheese and dark chocolates.

Julia and I compromised on the menu. I made my famous grilled vegetable salad and she whipped up her specialty, fried chicken. Even I couldn't resist.

I wanted to freeze this moment in time. All of my girls were happy and in assorted stages of lust and love. Derek and I were both. Our make-up sex was so *fuckaliscious* I nearly argued with him so we could make up again.

He was in LA auditioning a potential backup love interest for season six of *First Bite*. After the stunt Mandy Hamilton pulled at our engagement party, she went back into rehab. Her role was contingent on her sobriety. If she didn't complete rehab, the part would be recast. Derek asked me to go to LA with him. Even if I wanted to, I couldn't because of Brooke's party. It was a win-win for me. Although, the next time he asked, I would have to say yes. We worked hard finding the balance in our relationship.

Brooke opened all of her gifts except for Lacey and Sue's. Lacey presented her with the biggest heart-shaped *Godiva* chocolate I'd ever seen. Then Brooke held up Lacey's other gift, satin panties with a little heart on the bum.

"It's really a no-brainer," Lacey said. "If you wear panties with hearts on, Tom will have a hard-on."

We erupted with more laughter and the doorbell rang.

Sue leaped to her feet. "Brooke, my gift has just arrived."

*Holy heart stopper!* Sue purchased Brooke a special delivery, a Strip-O-Gram dressed as cupid. Now I knew where all the *Thunder from Down Under* rejects landed—in costumes of horrors, gyrating to "Open Your Heart" by Madonna.

We shrieked in hysterics. Brooke turned fifty shades of red while Cupid bobbled about. Nancy and Sharon grabbed the heart-shaped paper plates and spanked his diapered man ass. Then it happened, the diaper slipped and his bows and arrow sprang free. Brooke screamed as if she saw a spider, a super hairy, huge, floppy spider. Cupid turned to retrieve his britches and stuck his ass crack right in Brooke's face.

She yelled, "My eyes, my eyes."

We couldn't contain ourselves and convulsed in hilarity. Sammy, Coco, and Molly filed in the doggie door ready to pounce. Poor Cupid lost whatever shred of dignity he had left, but really, did he have to go commando? Sue ushered him out the door.

"Oh, Brooke, I'm so sorry. Are you okay?" Sue asked as she snatched up the wine and replenished our drinks.

Brooke took it like a champ. "I think I would've rather had a butt plug than Cupid's butt and arrow in my face."

Shannon chimed in, "I hope he's a shower and not a grower. Did you see the size of that thing?"

These girls didn't miss an opportunity to talk about sex. They grilled me about my bridal gifts. I confessed I wore the vibrating panties and the rest of the toys would not go to waste. I steered the conversation in Lacey and Shannon's direction and asked them about Jake and Walter. Lacey actually blushed. I thought she'd offer up juicy details. Both girls were tight-lipped, which told me they had fallen for these guys.

Phillip arrived and drove Julia and Coco home. Sammy stayed with Molly and me. She apologized for not staying to cleanup. Poor thing looked tired. I reminded her she was sleeping for two.

The rest of the husbands arrived one by one and collected their wives. I was glad no one drove home since we killed off some serious bottles of wine. Tom showed up last to take the guest of honor home. I'd like to see the look on his face when Brooke told him about the dangling Cupid. What would Derek say?

Lacey and Shannon were spending the night. They volunteered for cleanup duty, even though I preferred to do it myself.

Lacey asked sheepishly, "So, would it be all right if I slept in the downstairs master?"

"Well, you could, but that's where Jake sleeps when he stays."

As if on cue, Jake appeared in the kitchen. I teased, "Jake, Lacey asked if she could sleep in your room."

He responded in a serious tone, "If you or Mr. Pierce weren't comfortable with that I completely understand."

"It's totally fine. I was just giving you a hard time. Everyone is welcome here in whatever room they want to sleep in."

Poor Jake, I shouldn't have teased him, especially after he witnessed my naked roll and splat.

Lacey said, "Thanks, Nia. Oh, I almost forgot. Tomorrow I have a private with Jeff Peterson at six a.m. I know you set your alarm, but I don't want to wake Jake and those things confuse me. Is it okay to leave it off?"

"I'm fine with it, as long as Jake thinks it would be okay with Derek."

He said he thought it would be fine and they

headed off to bed. I was pretty sure they wouldn't be sleeping. Those two had chemistry for days.

Shannon exclaimed, "Jake is hot."

"Yeah, he has that whole biker, bad guy thing going on. He's actually a sweetheart. What about Walter? You didn't say much. What's been going on?"

"I didn't want to say it in front of everyone, but Walter and I slept together."

Too much information! "Um, wow, that's a lot for me to take in. I was thinking more along the lines are you officially dating?"

"I think so. I mean, I really like him and he's good in bed, not great, but he tries."

I wanted to jam my fingers in my ears and sing. "Okay, again, yikes, but I'm happy if you're happy."

"Yes, I'm happy."

"On that note, I'm going to go to bed. I put you in the guest bedroom next to the master. Are you coming up?"

"I think I'll stay down here for a bit and finish my wine. Walter's supposed to call and say good night."

"Okay, see you in morning."

Sammy, Molly and I snuggled in bed. I called Derek before I turned off the light. I was disappointed he was the same old distant LA Derek. The auditions didn't go well and he read the first episode of season six and hated it. When I asked him why he said we'd talk about it tomorrow when he flew back to Vegas. I didn't dare tell him about Cupid's floppy foot long freak show. Valentine's Day would never be the same.

I clicked through the TV stations and there was a *Subway* commercial, the one with the jingle, "Five-dollar footlong." It reminded me of Cupid, so I turned off the TV and went to sleep.

* * * *

I snapped out of a deep sleep with Sammy going berserk. He growled and barked. I flipped the light on. An eerie figure approached the bed and I screamed. Both dogs escalated in attack mode.

"It's me. Sorry, wrong room."

Jake burst through the door with his gun drawn.

"Don't shoot, it's me, Walter."

"Walter, what the fuck are you doing here?" I asked, and calmed down the dogs. Lacey and Shannon flew into room.

"I'm sorry. I meant to go to Shannon's room. I didn't mean to scare you?"

"You still didn't answer my question. What are you doing here? And how did you get in?"

Shannon confessed, "We were texting and I told him I'd unlock the back door if he wanted to come over."

"You left the door unlocked? You do realize that Jake is here for a reason. Is it still unlocked?"

Walter nodded and Jake took off. Shannon was beside herself with regret. "I'm sorry, I wasn't thinking clearly. I think I drank too much wine."

I could relate to that. "It's fine. Walter, you're welcome to stay."

Relief swept over both their faces. Walter approached the bed and Sammy snarled at him. He backed up. "Thank you. I guess I misunderstood Shannon's text."

Shannon and Walter retreated and Lacey flopped on the bed. "I don't believe him for a second."

"You don't believe he misunderstood Shannon's text?"

"No, I think he came into your room on purpose."

"Let's hope that's not true. Derek would shit if he found out Walter was in here. Do you think you could talk to Jake and convince him it's in both of our interests not to tell him?"

Before Lacey could answer, Jake strolled in the room and said in a firm tone, "No, she couldn't do that. We need to tell Mr. Pierce everything."

"I know you're right, but do we have to tell him everything? I mean, can't we skip naked Cupid?"

Lacey's eyes widened and she shook her head.

"Naked cupid?" Jake asked.

Well, wasn't that awesome, me and my big mouth. Poor Lacey had some explaining to do and I did too. Derek would not be pleased.

* * * *

"So, what you're telling me is Walter James waltzed into my house through an unlocked door?" Derek was pissed and had every right to be. He arrived home to Jake and me relaying our evening of shame. Jake took the blame.

I worried Derek would fire him. "Derek, this was more my fault than Jake's. I said anyone was welcome here. I didn't think Shannon would literally take me up on it, but she drank too much and wasn't thinking."

Jake interrupted, "Right, but if I had set the alarm this wouldn't have happened. I take full responsibility. It won't happen again."

Derek softened. "That was all I needed to hear, thank you."

Jake and I exchanged glances. Oh, man, just when I thought I was in the clear. One of us had to tell Derek about Cupid's droopy, dropped drawers.

I suppose it should be me. "Derek, there was an incident at the party I should probably tell you about."

"Well, if you don't need me for awhile, I have some errands to run." Jake was such a chicken shit. "Would you like me to drive you to your meeting with Martin, or stay here with Nia?"

"I'll drive myself. I'm sure Nia could use some alone time after last night. Take the rest of the day off."

Jake shot me a half grin and left. Derek asked, "What is it, sweetie? What happened at the party?"

"Well, you know how my shower was all butt plugs and nipple clamps?"

"Ah, yes, the gifts that keep on giving."

"Last night the theme was hearts and flowers. Sue purchased Brooke a little treat, only it wasn't so little."

"What was it?"

I said it all in one breath, like ripping off a *Band-Aid.* "It was a Strip-O-Gram, dressed as Cupid, and his diaper fell off and he was naked. It was so gross. I wish I could unsee it. Poor Brooke almost got poked in the eye."

He laughed. "My girl really knows how to throw a party. Come here, I missed you."

I dashed into his arms and he held me close. "You're not mad about stupid Cupid or Walter."

"No, baby, I'm just happy to be home. I need to talk to you about something."

"Can you hold me in the tub?"

"I would love to, my angel, but my meeting is in hour and this can't wait. Come."

He led me to the sofa and sat across from me on the coffee table. "Remember when I told you I read the script for the first episode, season six? I hate it because it's completely contrived. My character is doing things that don't make sense, just for ratings. They're pushing the envelope when it comes to nudity. I don't have a problem with it if serves the story, like season three, but this doesn't even come close."

"Will you be naked with Mandy, a lot?"

"Yes, and she's part of the problem. I've had enough issues on set with Oliver and Gisela. I don't need her showing up late with two sober coaches making demands."

"How do you know she'll do that?"

"I don't, it's just that I've already been told by the producers, whatever she wants she gets. They really think her playing my love interest will save the show and guarantee a seventh season. The ratings have been declining since season three. This could be the last year if they don't pick up, but in the first episode, Drake saves Mandy's character, Grace, from zombies, and then they have sex practically the entire episode."

My stomach knotted. "I know that this comes with the territory, but doesn't it seem a little extreme?"

Derek grasped my hands. "Yes. And that's why I want you in LA when we start shooting. I think it's what's best for us, especially the first episode."

"I don't think I can. We're going to Napa and then you start shooting. I can't miss that much work. It's not fair to Lacey."

"Can you at least think about coming to LA more often?"

Dr. Roma's voice echoed in my head telling me to meet him halfway. "Okay, I'll talk to Lacey, but I can't come back from Napa and then fly to LA the next day. I'll do what I can. I want to be there for you."

He smiled and cradled me on his lap. "Thank you. I hope you know how much I love you. This is going to be tough on both of us, but just hold on to me, sweetie, I won't ever let go."

# Chapter Twenty

The clock ticked. In less than forty-eight hours, we were flying to Napa. I was so excited I packed and repacked three times. It was a shame Julia couldn't sample the wine, but she looked forward to escaping the heat. Every time I envisioned the four of us floating around wine country, I did a happy dance in my head. It was something I dreamed of doing and Derek made it happen.

Now it was my turn to make something happen for him. When he strolled in the bedroom after his meeting, he would be treated to the surprise of his life. Yes, I dipped my toe back into the pool of spontaneity, only this time I hatched a plan.

I packed my bridal shower toys and outfits. Then I decided to grant Derek a sneak peek. After careful consideration, I donned the garters and stocking ensemble minus the panty. Derek would find me faced down on my knees, with my ass in the air at the edge of the bed. Next to me, he'd discover the lube and a toy. I named my spontaneous plan, the butt plug surprise.

If the devil was in the details, you could call me Satan. Molly was at Julia's, Jake was with Lacey, and my cell phone was in my hand. I wasn't taking any chances. I popped on a new pair of my killer heels and checked myself in the bathroom mirror. I never considered myself sexy, but I was so free and confident with Derek, somehow sexy oozed out of my pores.

My phone vibrated with Derek's text saying he'd be home in five minutes. It was show time. An immediate scorching sensation seared through my body. I placed my cell phone on the nightstand and examined my costar. The design made sense. The further it eased inside me the thicker it became. It would feel harder than Derek's finger. I wanted it. Maybe someday soon, he would have all of me. Just the thought produced a pool of liquid between my thighs.

I assumed my naughty ass in air the position. I was like an empowered bad girl in need of a spanking. My dripping sex begged to be taken. This was the longest five minutes of my life.

Derek's footsteps bounded up the stairs. He gasped and cleared his throat. "Um...I was expecting my sweet, innocent looking fiancée."

"Looks can be deceiving."

"That is the understatement of the year. Baby, you're beautiful." He splayed his hands on my ass and pressed his lips to my lower back. "Come here, let me look at you." He curved his arm around my waist and angled me toward him. His eyes soaked me in and he gave me that look, my look, the one that was for me alone.

He brushed his fingertips over my burning skin. "Whatever is going on in that devious head of yours, I'm all in. You look so fucking hot. Your body was made for sex. Your body was made for me, it's mine."

He seized my mouth and claimed what was his. Yes, I was his and he was mine. His kiss was so wild and heavenly at the same time. I drank in the sweetness of him as his demanding lips caressed mine. I was so aroused and I hadn't even produced the main attraction. He released me, and our breath was uneven and heavy.

I panted. "I have a surprise for you."

Derek's gaze landed on my costar and he let out an approving growl. "I've always said I like the way you think. I love you, Nia. And I said Nia, because I mean business."

I murmured, "I love you too."

He cupped my face. "My good girl, I know you need to come. Turn around, show me that pretty little ass of yours."

I resumed my ass in the air position. Derek's hands grazed my garters. "I love these. I think we'll leave them on."

His mouth lingered at my entrance, producing a tingle in the pit of my stomach. He blew lightly on my lustful pussy and every nerve ending fused with zeal. A small trickle of my juices released, and Derek filleted me open with his fingers.

My soft moans filled the air as he sprinkled me with gentle lashes of his tongue. His strokes intensified as he gorged himself with hearty mouthfuls of my drooling, plump pussy flesh. Then his tongue popped inside my luscious hole, stoking the burning fire. He milked me with utter supremacy. I reared back, forcing the velvety wonder further inside. My body quaked as he swirled my walls, whisking me into a lather.

"Ah, Derek, I can't, oh God."

He whispered, "Don't, sweetie. Don't hold back. Come for me."

Three fingers delved inside and quickly pumped me to the brink. Then Derek tapped my clit with ardent spanks. I burst like a rain cloud in monsoon season, and showered his hand with my spraying release while wailing in pleasure.

Derek grunted, "That's it, my baby, let it out."

One final shudder hit me and I collapsed on the bed. "Fuck, Derek, I don't know how you did that. I think we need rubber sheets. I'm spent."

If butt plug surprise was act two, I needed an intermission.

Derek lay on the bed next to me and calmed my flesh with the back of his hand. "That's okay. I plan on taking my time with you."

"You're still dressed?"

He palmed my right butt cheek. "I'm enjoying the

view. I love this perfect little curve of your bottom and the way your skin feels like silk. You're so sexy."

I sat up and climbed into his lap. "When you look at me like that, I feel sexy."

He graced my lips with a soft kiss and a smirk crossed his face.

"What's that look for?"

"I'm just trying to remember if you did anything naughty today?"

"Duh, did you not see my ass in the air when you walked in the room?"

"No, I mean did you do anything spank-worthy?"

"Well, give me a second. I'm sure I can come up with something."

I parted my lips and his tongue probed my mouth. Then I came up with it. A sure fire way to earn a spanking. I broke the kiss. "Hey, your birthday is next month. You know, when you'll be thirty-three years *old.*"

He shook his head. "Somebody wants a pink bottom." Instead of taking me over his knee, he hooked me under the knees and flipped them in the air. I screamed in delight.

His fingers skimmed along my taint. "I think this is an undiscovered wonderland." He was right, so many pleasure receptors waiting to be tapped. He spanked my bottom and his hand landed squarely on my crack crease inflaming my wonderland. My body ramped as he delivered quick chastening smacks to my willing ass. Derek licked the back of my kneecaps and a current fizzed on my clit.

"Oh, my God, Derek, that feels amazing."

He spread my legs and petted my anxious pussy. "Good girl, you feel ready. Get back on the edge of the bed for me. Give me your ass."

I scampered to the edge while Derek stripped. I heard him open the nightstand.

He placed Buzz next to the butt plug. "I thought we'd invite your friend to the party. I want you as relaxed as possible. Clear your mind and focus on my voice. Let me take you."

Just the sound of his voice sent a smoldering wave of fresh feverish moisture to my sex. Derek's fingers were like magic wands sacredly encouraging my wet folds.

"Baby, I'm going to prepare your ass with my finger. I need you to breathe and open up for me. If it hurts, tell me to stop. Are you sure this is what you want?"

Breathless, I answered, "Yes."

His lips endowed each cheek with a kiss. The lid on the lube clicked open and Buzz hummed on the lowest speed. He slid him slowly over my dewy clit as his fingertip touched my tightest tunnel. I exhaled and opened for him and he gradually pushed inside. A load groan released from the back of my throat. I pressed myself into the vibrator, demanding more friction and Derek stopped.

"Sweetie, I don't want you to come yet. Just give in to me. I've got you."

His hand calmed down my soaking flesh and I gave in to him. He administered more lube on my anus and my snuggest hole welcomed the invader inside. Yes, it was more intense than Derek's finger in a raw and wanton way.

"Are you okay, baby?"

"Oh, God yes, please, more."

He moved the plug in and out with gentle thrusts. This forbidden, scintillating sensation spirited me to the sizzling edge. My cunt juice drizzled down my thighs as he sliced my most sinful opening.

"Derek, I'm so close, please, fuck me."

His tip taunted my entrance. "You're doing so well, your ass loves this. And since you said 'please' like a good girl, I'm going to grant you your request. Just remember how much I love you, because I'm about to take you so rough, you'll think I don't."

"Please. I want it."

My greedy pussy sucked him inside. This was a once in a lifetime fuck. He filled me like never before.

"Fuck, sweetie, you're so much tighter. You feel

incredible."

I maximized the impact by meeting him stroke for stroke. I took everything he gave me, while his stony dick mass and the ass plug worked me into a quivering cluster of manic hysteria. He forced the bung stopper in all the way, and held it firmly in place. I shrieked like a carnal demon. Then he pummeled me with unprecedented cock thrusts that slaughtered my pussy. His untamed rally of torment wrenched me from end-to-end.

Our animalistic grunts and groans reached fever pitch as my release pelted me to a state of ravishment. My violent eruption set off Derek's implosion inside me. His mighty supply of hot cum jettisoned within like a geyser. Then he grabbed my plug with a final tug and a wicked spigot rushed forth. Our bodies writhed and shook in submission to the provocative pleasure. It was pure nirvana. We crashed on the bed, trembling in a sweaty clump of listless limbs. From out of nowhere, a sneeze snuck up on me and the jolt sent my butt plug hurling on the floor.

We cracked up and I said, "Now that was not sexy."

Derek pressed me against him and smoothed the hair off my face. "It was quite impressive, like you. Just when I think we can't reach new heights, you manage to amaze me."

Yes, the butt plug surprise received five stars. I would give it a twelve out of ten ranking. I mean, talk about pulling out all the stops.

Derek kissed my shoulder and padded to the bathroom. I was flat on my stomach reveling in bliss. I closed my eyes and Derek tended to me with a warm washcloth. Without a word, he applied lavender lotion to my bum and nestled me next to him. We were so peaceful. Then my phone vibrated.

Derek handed it to me. "I think you better answer it, it's Phillip."

"Hey, Phillip, what's up? Oh, my God, okay, yes, yes, we'll be right there."

"Sweetie, what is it?"

"It's Julia, she lost the baby."

# Chapter Twenty-One

"I'm so sorry." Julia sobbed uncontrollably in my arms. I'd never seen her so devastated and shattered. I understood her pain all too well. Phillip appeared helpless and shell-shocked.

"What happened?"

"I had a little spotting and I called my gynecologist. She told me it was probably nothing, but I could come and see her just to be safe. By the time I got there, I was cramping. She did an ultrasound and said the pregnancy was no longer viable. It's like it vanished, and she made it sound like I was never pregnant in the first place. But I was, and I already loved my baby. It was everything to me."

A fresh set of tears flooded her eyes. I held her hand. "I know. I loved your baby too."

"I'm so glad you're here. I told Phillip not to call you. I thought it would be too hard on you because of… I'm just glad you're here."

"There isn't anywhere else I'd rather be, than right by your side. Do you want me to call your parents?"

"Oh, God no, they are the last two people I want to talk to."

Julia had a complicated relationship with her parents. They divorced when she was an infant and both made careers of choosing the worse mates and divorcing them too. She had more half and stepsiblings than she could count. They weren't close. They were the kind of mom and dad that were generous with their checkbook, and not with their time or attention. It was one of the reasons we bonded so fast. We were like orphans in our families.

She dabbed her eyes. "I'm really sorry, but I can't go to Napa. The Doctor said I need to take it easy for a week."

"Of course you can't go and we aren't going either, right Derek?"

Derek and Phillip joined us on the sofa in the TV room. Derek responded, "Whatever you need Julia, we're here for you, for both of you."

Phillip drew Julia to him. "We don't want you to miss your trip. I'll promise I'll take good care of Julia."

"Are you kidding? We aren't going anywhere. I'm going to sit on this couch with you until you're sick of me."

We stayed until Julia said she was ready to turn in for the night.

When we arrived home, I fled upstairs and out to the balcony. I searched for my star. The Almach shone bright that night. I said a prayer for Julia and Phillip and I asked my parents to watch over their baby and the baby I lost too. Seeing Julia in agony transported me to my darkest time. It was a deep loss you never got over. You just learned to live with it. I asked God to help me in the coming days to comfort Julia.

Derek joined me, and cradled me in his arms. "Did you come out here to find your star?"

I pointed to the heavens. "I did. Look, it's right there."

He kissed my temple. "Are you doing okay? This must be hard on you."

"It is, but when I had my miscarriage Julia never left my side. I want to do the same thing for her. I hope you're not upset about Napa."

"Sweetie, of course not, actually it might work out better this way. I was wondering if you could switch schedules with Lacey. You could cover her shifts this week since we aren't going out of town and then next week you could come to LA with me."

His idea threw me for a loop. Derek held me tighter. "I know I'm springing this on you. You don't have to give me an answer right now. Just think about it for me."

I nodded. Derek caressed my face. "Thank you, my angel. Let's get you in bed. It's been a hell of day."

We climbed in bed and I tucked into my regular spot on Derek's chest, except I was practically on top of him. The weight of the day took its toll and a few tears escaped.

Derek kissed the top of my head. "Hey, my angel, look at me. I know you will always mourn the loss of your baby, but one day I hope we will have babies together. I want that if you still do."

"I do want that, wait, did you say babies? Exactly how many were you thinking?

"Oh, I don't know, but I keep imagining a little girl with dark hair, an adorable face, and a smart mouth."

"You mean you want two of me?"

"I'd take ten of you if I thought I could handle it."

"You could try."

"Right now, I'm happy with the one in my arms. Goodnight, my sweet girl, I love you."

* * * *

The next day Julia and I hunkered down on the sofa and binge watched old school style. *The Carol Burnett Show* and *Andy Griffith* produced some serious belly laughs. Laughter was indeed the best medicine. Julia was still in her pajamas, but she made progress.

I brought over my juicer and made her favorite, apple, carrot, and ginger. At first, the sad fog in her eyes lifted, but when I returned from the kitchen, a vacant expression crossed her face.

She turned to me. "I need to apologize to you."

"Apologize, what for?"

"I feel like I was a terrible friend when you had your miscarriage."

"What are you talking about? You literally saved my life and helped me start over."

"What I mean is, emotionally all I could do was sympathize. I didn't understand what it was like to be in your shoes. I should've been there for you more. Sometimes I think of all the practical things and not the emotional ones. I hope you can forgive me."

I embraced her. "Oh, my God, Julia, there is nothing to forgive. No one can understand this pain unless they go through it too. I'm just sorry you have to. It's not fair."

Tears spilled down her cheeks. "I feel like a mother without a baby."

"But you will be a mother. You will be the best mother in the entire world. You and Phillip are destined to be parents. I know it."

"Do you really think so?"

"I know so. Plus, look at it this way. Now I have time to catch up. Wouldn't it be fun to be pregnant together? I'd like to see how Derek and Phillip would deal with that."

She giggled. "Good point. Thank you for making me laugh and being here. You really are my sister. I love you."

"I love you too, sis."

* * * *

Over the next few days, Brooke and I took turns hanging out on Julia's sofa, and feeding her all her favorites. Derek kept Phillip occupied on the golf course, even though he sucked at it. Lacey switched schedules with me, but I hadn't made up my mind about LA. My focus rested squarely on Julia.

Four days into her healing, Julia, Brooke, and I glued in to a *Desperate Housewives* marathon. Unfortunately, we stumbled upon an episode where one of the characters had a miscarriage.

I seized the remote and turned it off. "Maybe we should watch something else."

Brooke interjected. "I need to tell you both something. I've actually never told anyone. When I was married to my ex, I had a miscarriage too. It was very early, but it was awful."

Julia and I comforted Brooke. She was close to tears. "Look, as the older wiser gal here. I'm going to give you both some advice. Julia, whatever you do, don't shut Phillip out. I did that. Our sex life was consumed with baby making. After my miscarriage, I didn't want to have sex for a long time. And when we did, I wasn't present. I don't blame him for the affair. In a way, it was my fault. I wasn't a good wife."

"That's not true." Julia said. "You can't blame yourself for what he did."

"I do, though. I just don't want you to make the same mistake I made."

"I won't and thank you."

Now it was my turn for Brooke's advice. "Nia, you're not going to want to hear this, but I think you should go to LA with Derek. If he needs you then you need to be there for him."

"You're right. I didn't want to hear that."

"Wait, I'm not finished. I think you should leave Molly with me and spend a couple days with Derek alone, and then I'll fly out with Molly and join you. That way, if he becomes LA Derek you have someone to hang out with. Plus, I've always wanted to go to Rodeo Drive and Grauman's Chinese Theatre."

"Oh, good plan, I'm with Brooke. You should go to LA. Don't be a wuss."

"I'm not being a wuss. I just haven't decided yet. A part of me thinks if I'm not in LA when he shoots naked sex scenes with Mandy Hamilton they aren't actually happening. It would be so much easier on me."

"Maybe it's not about you, maybe it's about what Derek needs," Julia said. "You have to admit, if you asked for the moon he would try to give it to you. Didn't Dr. Roma say for you to strive for more balance? Brooke's plan is perfect and you know it."

"Geez, were you like, in my therapy session?" My two besties ganged up on me. "Fine, I'll go to LA. I do love a good plan, so thank you, Brooke, it is perfect."

"Beverly Hills, here I come. Thank you, I've been so lonely while Tom's been gone, this will be good for me too. Speaking of which, if it's okay with Julia, I think we should watch the rest of this episode. Gabi does something at the end of the show to give her closure. That's the hardest part about having a miscarriage. It's such a huge loss, but there's no funeral, no anything."

I replied, "I know. It's easy to be stuck in the well.

For me it felt like I was at the bottom of the well with no way out of my deep dark hole of grief."

Julia quietly said, "Then I think we should watch it."

We held hands and watched the episode. At the end, Gabi released a pink balloon in honor of the baby she miscarried. For such a tongue-in-cheek show, this was a powerful moment.

All of us shed a few tears. Then Julia clicked off the TV and stood. "We need to do that, the three of us, together."

* * * *

The next day we gathered in Julia's backyard with pink balloons. Derek, Phillip, and the dogs joined us. In silence, we joined hands and released our balloons one at a time. It also released a deep ache I carried in my soul. While I wouldn't forget the tiny angel I never held in my arms, there was closure, there was peace.

# Chapter Twenty-Two

"Derek, they're beautiful, thank you so much." I was in LA, in Derek's kitchen. He filled the entire house with vases of white hydrangeas. There was no doubt about it. I would walk down the aisle with a bouquet of hydrangeas.

I plucked a bushel from its vase and sang the wedding march, mimicking a walk down the aisle. He grinned in that Derek way that sent my heart soaring. We were getting married on Christmas Eve. This incredible man was going to be my husband.

I stood on my tiptoes and pressed my lips to his, "I do, Mr. Pierce, I really do."

He gripped me to him. "You'll do nicely. We need to get you naked. I have another surprise for you."

"A late midnight surprise? Yes, surprises are my thing."

"I never thought I'd hear you say that."

"I didn't see it coming myself."

He took the flowers from me and tossed them off. He caressed my face and granted me a kiss, my kiss. The one that was full of love and laced with heat and yearning. It was mine. I was lost in him from the moment our eyes met. We were lost to each other from the moment our lips joined, in that first kiss.

His phone rang.

"Derek, don't answer it, please, don't."

"I'm sorry, sweetie, I have to. Hello, this is Derek... Oh, hey, no, it's fine. Yes, I'm looking forward to working with you. Mandy, it's going to be great."

Did he really break our kiss to talk to Mandy Hamilton? Derek shrugged and motioned for me to go upstairs.

I tromped upstairs in disbelief. I'd been in LA all of three seconds before something went wrong. That shouldn't have been a surprise.

I sulked in bed and waited for Derek. An hour was long enough. I turned out the light and went to sleep.

* * * *

"Baby, wake up, my sweet girl."

I rolled over and his sorrowful eyes met my angry ones. "I shouldn't have come."

"I'm so glad you did. I'm sorry about last night. The last thing I want to do is be on the phone to Mandy, she bugs the crap out of me."

"Then why were you?"

He sighed. "I'm under a lot of pressure from the producers. Like I said, anything she wants she gets."

I looked down. "Does that mean you too?"

Derek's finger tipped my chin to face him. "No, I am yours and yours alone. It's just Mandy's sobriety is hanging by a thread. She's really insecure about acting again. I've been asked to be there for her and hold her hand. She's one meltdown away from rehab."

"Doesn't she have an understudy?"

"Yes, but she's an unknown, and won't get the same buzz Mandy will. If Mandy goes back to rehab the show might be finished."

"Would that be the worst thing?"

"No, not for me, but for everyone else, I've got try to make it work."

"Does she really bug the crap out of you?"

"Fuck yes, she's the most annoying person I've ever been around."

I giggled. "Wow, I've never heard you say that before."

"Trust me, acting like her new best friend is the best acting I've done in my entire life. I should get an Academy Award."

He drew me onto his lap. "Am I forgiven?"

His lips touched my forehead and I melted in his arms. "Yes, you're forgiven. I'm just going to miss you when you're on set. I don't know what I'll do with myself."

"I'll leave Bernie with you. He can take you wherever you want to go."

"That's the problem, honey, I don't know where anything is."

"Well, today won't be a long day. I'm rehearsing with Mandy before the table read tomorrow. Lunch is at one, and then depending on how it goes, I could be finished early. I'll be home by six at the latest. Tomorrow I can send Keith to entertain you, would you like that?"

"Yeah, he's fun to shop with."

"Done, and then Brooke will be here with Molly. Sound like a plan?"

I kissed his cheek. "That is an excellent plan."

"Sweetie, I'm just getting warmed up. I was thinking how much I would love to come home to you, and the very first dinner you ever made for me. The salad with the mango and avocado and the prawns with your juices redistributing, I loved it."

"You've got yourself a deal. But I'd have to go to the store."

"That's the best part. I'll have Bernie take you to Frescos. They have all that organic stuff you love, miles of kiwi and kale."

I grinned. "I do love a nice grocery store."

He lips graced mine with a soft kiss. "That's, my girl. Hmm… I almost forgot about your surprise."

He reached into the top drawer of his nightstand and produced a fancy package. "I'm spoiling you, and no arguments."

Was that what I thought it was? "Derek, a *Rolex*? You fucking didn't?"

"I fucking did. Do you like it?"

"It's a *Rolex…* It's—"

"It's platinum, actually."

His smile beamed with sheer jubilation. I wasn't going to argue and say it was too much. Instead, I showed my sheer over-the-top, over the moon excitement.

"I love it. It's the most amazing watch in the world, and you are the sweetest, most generous, most perfect man, ever. Thank you. I love you."

He slipped the watch on my wrist. It sparkled and shined. "I love you too."

His mouth swooped down to capture mine. He ignited me with a series of slow shivery kisses.

He whispered, "You didn't argue with me, so I'm not going to spank you."

"You're not?"

His lips embraced my neck with growing desperation. "I didn't have to say I insist, either, so I'm not going to fuck you."

I heaved. "What are you going to do?"

"I'm going to make love to my gorgeous fiancée."

He cradled me in his arms and laid me on the bed. His gaze swept over my naked body in adoration. His face held that same expression of desire, just like the first time he saw me spread out on the bed.

Our eyes met. "Nia Kelly, you are the most beautiful woman on earth."

He sealed his body on top of mine, flesh against flesh, his weight sinking me deep into the bed. He pinned his arms on top of mine with our fingers intertwined.

I opened for him, and with one effortless stroke, his cock glided inside my slippery channel. I glowed in the warmth of him from head to toe. He submerged himself fully, swaying me slow and easy, indulging my lips with steamy, hot kisses. I simmered under his control. I was his for the taking.

I was his.

Derek released my arms, and his hand cupped my face. "I love you, my angel."

My fingers tangled in his hair and I drew him to my mouth. "I love you too."

I held onto his broad shoulders as he invigorated the heat torching us within. My entire being took in everything about him. The way his eyes penetrated me with everlasting lust and love, his scent that enlivened my senses, enraging my longing, even the hairs on his body tickling my skin, causing it to break out in goose bumps. I feasted my eyes on his powerful, rippling body. The way his muscles tensed and flexed as he drove us to rapture.

His cock grazed my sweet spot and my walls stirred around him. We percolated in pleasure.

He whispered, "My sweet girl, you feel amazing."

His strokes grew more fervent. I bent my knees, and pressed my feet into the bed and met his potent thrusts. Fierce fiery sensations resonated to my core. I felt every inch, every contour of him, enriching our awaited bliss.

Derek hooked his arms around my knees, lifting

my bottom off the bed. "Wrap your legs around me, sweetie."

He inched to his knees and skewered me to the root. My pussy reeled and sobbed on his cock. Once again, Derek was taking us to heights beyond heaven's gate. He thrashed into me and I cried out his name, yearning for more.

"Not yet, baby, just breathe, breathe with me."

He calmed our pace and we breathed together. It was the breath of life, uniting us for eternity.

He rocked us with an interlude of enthralling, fluid strokes, while I was spellbound at the site of him sliding in and out of me.

My inner muscles locked around his massive column, as he renewed his erotic, sultry motion. The pressure boiled inside me like a wild fire. My body bowed in fervent urgency. Convulsing in moans of frantic elation, I threw my head back.

"Nia, your eyes. I need your eyes. Look at me."

I gazed into his eyes, his very soul. His hand reached for mine, our palms pressed together as one, and we came. We rode the crest of our sweet release as it emerged and descended through us. We did it together.

Pure euphoria fell over us. He lowered me to the bed and delivered reverent kisses to my lips. If only we could stay in our bubble all day.

We expelled soft exhales into each other's mouths. His finger traced my hairline and flowed down to my jaw.

His eyes held me in wonderment. "Sweetie, you are exquisite. That was incredible."

"It was so good, I may never argue with you again."

He smiled. "That'll be the day. I don't buy that for a second."

I twirled my fingers in his hair. "I suppose my butt would be awful lonely if it didn't get a little punishment once in a while."

"I suppose my hand would squirm if it didn't get to spank your perfect bottom from time to time."

"Well, we can't have that. By the way, I have another butt plug-ish surprise for you."

He cocked his head in delighted curiosity. "Butt plug-ish, is that like butt plug, adjacent?"

I giggled. "Something like that. I brought the rest of my bridal shower gifts."

His eyes lit up. "You brought all of them, and the outfits too?"

"Yes, we have vibrators and handcuffs and nipple clamps, oh my! Surprise!"

He chuckled. "You have my permission to surprise me any time?"

"The real question is where do we begin?"

"Hmm…there is something appealing about having you handcuffed without any control, like my little sex slave."

I brought his lips to mine. "Sounds like an

excellent plan."

Below his cock released me a little and I grasped him tight. "Derek please, please stay, stay inside me a little longer."

"Baby, I have to shower, I've got to get to set."

From out of nowhere, tears pricked my eyes. "Please, five more minutes."

The pad of his thumb wiped them away. "Hey, what's all this?"

"I don't know, I can't explain. I just need you to stay."

"Of course, I'm right here. I'll stay."

* * * *

After Derek left, I worked out in his gym. The endorphins kicked out my funk from earlier. What was that? For some reason I couldn't let him go.

I showered and got ready to hit Frescos with Bernie when struck with a brilliant plan. Derek said I could surprise him anytime. I had a doozie. Instead of prawns and salad for dinner, he would have prawns and salad for lunch, in his trailer on set. His lunch break was at one, I had just enough time.

I called Keith. "Hey, Keith, it's me, Nia."

"Hey, baby doll, welcome back to the land of crazy and crazier."

"Thanks, I was wondering if you could help me get on set today. I have a surprise for Derek."

His voice sounded funny. "I don't know. Mandy might not like a guest on set for her first day. Everyone is walking on egg shells."

"Oh no, trust me, I do not want to lay eyes on her after she spilled wine on me at my engagement party. Derek said his lunch break is at one. I thought I'd surprise him with a picnic and then I'll leave. I wanted to make sure I could get on the lot. Can you help me?"

"Sure, is Bernie bringing you or did you decide to really surprise Derek and drive his Lamborghini."

"Can you imagine? I think I'll pass. I'm in no mood for a Lamborghini lecture. I'll stick with Bernie."

"Okay, I'll leave a pass at the security gate. Do you remember which studio and how to get in?"

"Yes, it's Studio 10, the grey door on the left side."

"Yep, you got it."

"Oh and, Keith, don't say a word to Derek, promise? I want him to be surprised."

"Not a peep, I won't even be here, but I will see you tomorrow for our shopping spree."

"Thanks, you're the best."

* * * *

I was in the back seat of Derek's big black car with my picnic basket. Derek was right. The grocery store was awesome. Hmm…maybe LA wasn't so bad.

We just pulled through security. Bernie found a spot close to the studio and I hopped out with my surprise in tow.

"Thanks for the lift. I'll be back in about an hour."

"You're welcome, Miss Kelly. It was my pleasure."

Nervous jitters danced in my stomach when I entered the studio. There weren't nearly as many people milling about like last time. I remembered the way to Derek's trailer and embarked on the short journey. My prawns and salad would be a welcome change from grabbing something from the commissary and eating in his trailer alone. Today was his treat.

I stood at the door and eased the handle down slow. *If he doesn't hear the door, he'll be even more surprised, like I appeared from thin air.*

The handle didn't make a sound. The door crept open and...*no!* Mandy was in Derek's trailer. They were kissing. Their lips unlocked and she peeled off her top. Derek smiled in delight at her full, ample mounds. His hand caressed her face. He gave her that look—my look.

I dropped the basket and clasped my hands to my face. "Oh, my God."

Derek's head snapped toward me. "Nia!"

I spun and fled for the grey door with tears streaming down my face. I was a fool, an absolute fool for coming here. I was even a bigger fool for believing in happy endings.

Derek chased me and cried out, "Nia, wait. It's not..."

When I got outside, Derek put me in a bear hug and I kicked and jerked under his grip. "Derek, let go me."

He held me up against the wall. "Will you stop for one second and let me explain."

I yelled, "There's nothing to explain, I saw with my own two eyes."

He got in my face and gritted. "You have to calm down. You're causing a scene. I can fix this, but not now."

I sobbed. "You can't fix anything. I'm going to back to Vegas."

His stare bore down on me. "No, you're not. You are not running away from me again."

"I can't stay here. Not after what I saw."

"God damn it, Nia, we were rehearsing over lunch because that's what she demanded."

"So that's how it's going to be? You rehearse naked in your trailer. It's disgusting. This whole thing is disgusting. I'm leaving."

"Fuck, you just don't get it."

"Oh I get it. There's always going to be a model or an actress or a psychopath in a Porsche. It's never going to change." My body shook under a torrent of tears. "You didn't even say you were sorry." I covered my face and wept.

He hands touched mine and I jerked away. His voice softened. "Of course, I'm sorry. We can fix this, I'll fix it."

I shook my head and cried, "No, no, no!"

"Nia, don't say that. Don't leave. Promise me you'll still be there when I get home tonight."

My body trembled and ached. I couldn't say anything. He removed my hands from my face. His eyes gripped with fear. "Promise me."

My jaw quivered and I gave a faint nod of my head. I promised him.

* * * *

On the ride back, the images of Mandy and Derek plagued my head. Their kiss, the way Derek smiled when he eyed her breasts and the look.

He gave her my look.

What would've happened if I hadn't showed up? What would happen tomorrow or next week? It was always something. Was I supposed to spend the rest of my life like this? Wondering when the next woman would come between us, and worrying if he would succumb to the temptation one day.

I loved Derek so much, but I loved myself too. I couldn't lose myself in his life. The clear realization crushed me. I couldn't live like this.

Back at the house, I booked a one-way ticket and packed my bag. I would keep my promise to Derek, I would be here when he returned, but I was leaving, leaving him, leaving us.

I sat my bag down in the kitchen. I took off the Rolex and placed it on the island next to the white hydrangeas. My fingertips touched the petals. They were delicate and fragile. They were like us.

I looked at my engagement ring. When he asked me to marry him, it was the happiest day of my life. It wasn't supposed to end like this. It wasn't supposed to end at all. Anguish and anger gripped me. I grabbed the vase of flowers, and smashed it on the floor.

Heaving sobs thrashed my body. I slipped off my ring. Through my tears, I stared at it on the island, touched it one last time and sunk to the floor. My body lay quaking.

The sound of crackling glass startled me. It was Derek tramping on the broken shards.

I hoisted myself off the ground. Transfixed we stared at one another. Oh God, I loved him. I loved him, but I didn't have any fight left in me. I loved him. In my head, I cried out, "Please, Derek, say something. I'm giving up. Please, say something."

His gaze fell on my ring. He didn't utter a word.

He let go…


**THE END**


Nia and Derek's journey continues in *A Way Back,* book three of the Swept Away trilogy…

# A Way Back
## *Swept Away, Book 3*

The battle to trust and communicate, fan the flames in Nia and Derek's over-heated relationship. Their only solace is the exploration of each other's sensual desires. It's their way, a way back to one another.

Their world is further complicated by the constant threat to Nia's safety. There is a traitor in their midst. Friendships are tested and damaged. Nia's choices set off and avalanche of explosive consequences.

Their road to freedom and happiness is rough and terrifying, but it is the only way home.

# Author Biography

Rosemary grew up in Pennsylvania, one of six children. Her parents, Charles and Dorothy, always supported all her creative endeavors, from acting to singing to Erotic Novelist. Yes, they are super cool.

She's been living in Las Vegas for over eighteen years with her husband Bill Johnson and their rescued pooch Harley.

In addition to writing, she also teaches ten fitness classes a week. Her limited spare time is usually spent at home with her hubby enjoying a home cooked, healthy meal and all things HBO and Netflix. When she ventures out to a restaurant, she normally splurges on her favorite dish, Mac and Cheese. It's just like Nia says in, the Swept Away series, "Sometimes it's good to be bad!"

# ROSEMARY WILLHIDE